Chapter 1

Al kept hearing the phone ringing constantly.

Damn man I wish whoever that is calling me will hang the fuck up, man damn I'm trying to sleep, they   see I ain't answering, Al thought to himself.

Whomever was calling hung up, and he instantly fell back asleep.....

Fifteen minutes later the phone started ringing again, breaking his peaceful sleep.

What the fuck, who the fuck is this calling me, Al thought to himself.

After about ten rings he just said fuck it, and went on and answered.

"Hello," Al said. "Wake your lazy ass up," K.P said.

"Man what the fuck you doing calling me this early in the morning, you know I got to go to school, in a couple of hours," Al said as he looked at the clock. "It's six in the morning," Al said. "Man she over here, she ready for us," K.P said enthusiastically.

His sleepy angry mode instantly changed.

"For real, she over there, okay I'm on my way," Al said.

"A'ight I'll talk to you when you get over here," K.P said as they both hung up.

He took a shit, and shower, get dressed, put on some cologne, swiftly made him some bacon and eggs, as he left out the door.....

After eating on his walk to his guy house he rolled up a fat joint out of his brown, back dime blazed it up and begin to puff inhaling and exhaling the potent weed smoke.....

K.P lived around the way, a few blocks over so he made it over his house within the matter of minutes.....

The one joint he smoked was a bomb, had him high as a kite, feeling a great sense of pleasurable delight.

He rang the doorbell, K.P instantly opened the door.

He walked into his guy house smelling the burning of sweet incense. Him and K.P walked to the kitchen and there she was sipping on cheap wine out of a plastic disposable cup. Smiling looking like a superstar, with her mini afro picked out, as her caramel skin glisten as the sunlight, with a smile that would make most men happy just seeing her.

This was Al's third time seeing her but this time she looked better than the other times, she looked wonderful.....

She shook his hand and greeted him in a professional way as if they were on the verge of conducting a top-flight business transaction.

K.P grabbed her by the hand gently walked her to the bedroom. Al went and sat on the couch which was in the living room positioned so he could see in the bedroom.

That was the plan for him to sit on the couch and watch them for a little while before he came and joined in, this was here first time running a train and she was kinda shy.

As K.P stood straight up she got on her knees and begin sucking his dick. Shortly he got on his knees, and she got on all fours and started back sucking his dick. Al entered the room got undressed quick, fast, and in a hurry and tried to stick his dick in her ass she stopped sucking K.P dick and said hold on that's the wrong hole, so he put it in her pussy, the pussy was a bomb, but it had a slight aroma to it in which he liked.

As the moisture of the pussy intensified his high, and made his dick feel amazing as he in and out her pussy he adored the way her ass jiggled in no time he was busting a nut in her pussy, coincidently all three of them were cumming at the same damn time, how great.

After K.P nutted in her face he started hitting it from the back as Al started getting his dick suck, switched up.

Once K.P nutted in her pussy he went to bathroom Al went back into her pussy from the back because her mouth was good, but couldn't make him nut. In no time he began to hear her yelling I'm cumming, I'm cumming, I'm cumming which was new to him, he had never had a female tell him when she was cumming.

He nutted in her. K.P came out the bathroom Al had just finished nutting so he got out the way as K.P went in her, talking dirty to her forcing the dick in and out the pussy.....

They realized that time had slipped past, and they needed to be on the move or they'd be late for the first day of school.

They nasty ass didn't even wash up they put they clothes on and left out. She went to a different school, so she went her separate ways from the guys in which went to the same school.....

It was September 4th 1976, it was the first day of school, the guys went to Cougar High.

Al and K.P. and some of their other homies stood in front of school getting their smoke on awaiting, the freshmen girls, they called them fresh meat.....

Al was a Junior and a thoroughbred on the Ho's; that's all he did was chase up behind Ho's.....

As the first day of school continued on Al bumped a gang of Ho's; not just Freshmen, but the Freshmen, Sophomores, Juniors, and Seniors. Shit he even came at a few of the new female teachers.....

That year, first semester, 6th period Al signed up for a music class. By it being the first day of school and first time taking a music class Al had no idea that this music class would be the shit.....

After 5th period lunch Al went to music class.....

Once he stepped into the classroom, he instantly noticed that the class was filled with 9th, 10th, 11th, and even 12th graders. This was odd to him. He'd never took a class with students of all different grade levels; all throughout high school all the other classes he'd took was designed for students that were in the exact same grade.

As the music class began the instructor introduced herself, and begin giving a lecture on what the music class would consist of.....

"Hello students, my name is Mrs. Miller, and I'll be your music teacher for this semester. Today I'll inform you on the basis of what my class consist of. This class will teach you how to play various musical instruments, primarily the Piano through music signs and graphs. Also, if a student has a talent as far as singing or reciting poetry you'll be able to do so once a week on Fridays into an open mic connected to a two way splitter united to a speaker and a tape recorder. As I'm sure everyone knows the speaker is so the class can hear vividly. The tape recorder is so you can listen to the recordings on the tape in the privacy of your own home to see for yourself if you need improvement or not. Without music certain events would've never took place. Many of you would've never been born without music; through the midst of love songs certain individuals mom and dad had sexual relations which resulted in the birth of some of you," Mrs. Miller said as the class begin laughing.

As Mrs. Miller continued on with her lecture Al begin to look around the class impatient for the class to be over for the day.

He began to look at this girl on his right side as she began looking at him as their eyes caught contact with each other at the same time.

They both became in a trance by one another's beauty; it was like love at first sight.

During the rest of the time while music class was pending they both continued to look at one another with a lustful glare in their eyes; neither one of them said a word to each other; they didn't want to disrupt the class.....

Once the class was over Al approached her to introduce himself.....

As Al walked towards her it was as if he was gliding on ice. It was as if the world and everyone in it besides him, and her had paused for a moment of time.

As Al became face to face with her he cleared his throat and introduced himself....."Hey, how are you doing, my name Al." "I'm doing alright, my name Joanne." "Joanne, shake my hand, be my friend open your booty and let me in," Al said as they both begin laughing.

"Sitting next to you in class I couldn't take my eyes off you, you just look so damn good to me," Al said, as she began smiling.

"Girl who you fuck with," Al asked? "I'm not fucking with nobody, I don't have a boyfriend," she said.

They talked for a few minutes about average shit, until Al realized that they had to go to their seven-period class.

"Listen right, you know we gotta go to our seven period classes, but I'll be waiting on you after school at 2:30," Al said. " A'ight I'll see you at 2:30," she said.....

They went their separate ways; both were stuck in a trance, like when boy meets girl, when woman meets man. The rest of their time in school they couldn't stop thinking of each other.

Once the school bell rang at 2:30 Al rushed out of the school to make sure he caught Joanne coming outta the school's front door.

While he stood in front of the school anxiously awaiting on Joanne to come out many others crossed his path, a few even tried to strike up a conversation with him, he paid them no attention. His focus was on one thing, Joanne!

Although he'd only talked to Joanne for a few minutes after class, he was really digging her, she was a bad chick.

As Al stared at the school's front door in a daze Joanne slowly walked out in the midst of the crowd of other students looking for him.

Al spotted her in the midst of the crowd he inherited a smile that was of joy and happiness, such a wonderful bliss.

He approached her smiling, striding in a pimpish walk form as if he were gliding on ice.

"Could I give you a ride home," Al asked? "Hell naw my momma and daddy would kill me if they see me getting outta the car with you," Joanne replied. "Why would they kill you for getting outta the car with me," Al asked? "My momma and daddy are religious to the third power, and I can't have boyfriends; I can't even be around boys without them there," Joanne said. "Well can I drop you off around the corner from your house," Al said. "Thanks, but no thanks I don't want to get into the car with a stranger," Joanne said. "Girl, I ain't no motherfucking stranger," Al said, as they both begin laughing. "Naw I didn't mean it like that, it's just that I don't wanna get into the car with someone I just met," she said.

"Do you live in the hood," Al asked? "Yeah I live on rush street," she replied. "Can I at least walk you home, I wanna kick it with you even if it's only for a little while," Al said.

Joanne began smiling and shaking her head up and down as a sign of yes.

As he began walking her home she immediately began to open up to him.....

"You know I ain't never had a boyfriend before," she said.

She's a virgin, and if I ever get some of that pussy I'm gonna tear that shit up, Al thought to himself.

"I hope that one day I can be your boyfriend," Al said.

She began to smile, thinking to herself I'd love that.

As they continued to walk and talk Al began to think to himself that by all means necessary Joanne would become his.

Al possessed a rare quality that a lot of the other players didn't possess; which was he'd first capture the Ho's heart and mind; he knew that once he got a Ho locked mentally, she'd do anything for him.

That's exactly what he was attempting to do capture Joanne's heart and mind.

Al looked Joanne in her eyes and told her, "you look fantastic." "You ain't all that bad yourself," Joanne replied, as they both begin laughing.

Al stopped walking, bent over to get something outta his sock. Joanne stopped walking and started looking at him like he was crazy and asked," boy what you doing." "I'm getting something outta my sock."

Al swiftly converted the conversation.....

"Get a pen and paper outta your bookbag, and take my number down," he said.

She took his number down, and told him, "you know I can't give you my number cuz my mom and dad would be tripping if you called me, but don't worry I'll make sure to call you when I get alone," Joanne said.

Al then came outta his sock with a brown bag dime of weed. He kept it in his sock just in case he had ever got searched by the police, it was rare that the police would look into someone's sock in search of illegal shit.

Then he stuck his hand in his pocket and pulled out some top papers and began rolling the weed up.

This whole ordeal was new to Joanne. She was kinda shy and didn't wanna seem like the lame she was.

After Al rolled up a joint, he placed it on the outside of his ear as they started back walking and talking.

She began talking about school, classes she'd like to take in the future, and goals after high school, such as college, and writing books of romance novels.

Al vividly listen to Joanne, her voice was like music to his ears.

Al put flame to the weed with his cigarette lighter.

Due to the smell of the weed Joanne now knew what he had rolled up.

She'd never seen no one roll weed up before, but she'd knew the smell, because when she was in grammar school she'd caught a few of her classmates smoking on the yard before, and asked them about it.

Joanne paused boldly stating, "you a dope fiend."

Al began laughing, "girl I ain't no damn dope fiend, this is Ses you understand me."

"What is Ses," she asked? "Ses is the best marijuana known to men." "Marijuana, that's still drugs," she said. "It's drugs but it ain't nothing like dope," he said.

As they continued to step slowly down the street he began to play games with the smoke which appeared amazing to her.

He'd take a pull off the joint, inhaling the smoke; then exhaling the smoke outta his mouth, back in his nostrils, then exhaling outta of his nose.

She really liked his demeanor. Al was super cool, a straight player.

"This is the furthest you can walk me, I live right around the corner; I'll call you a little later on if my parents leave, and go to the grocery store or something.

If I don't call you don't get the wrong idea thinking I'm being phony. If I don't call you that means my parents never left," she said. "I know," he said.

"You steady saying parents like you from the suburbs or something, "he said, as they both begin laughing, and went their separate ways.....

Al normally didn't stay in the house, but he did this particular day anxiously awaiting on Joanne to call. Each time the phone rang he'd frantically answer it, hoping it was Joanne. She never called that day.

As Joanne went to sleep that night, she had an intense dream that was so life like that it made her awake from her sleep; she had a dream that Al and her kissed throughout a summer's night as Al pulled her tittys out and sucked it as breast milk flowed in his mouth she continued to breast feed him.

The next day at school Joanne and Al were able to kick it before school started, after music class, and after school to.

Within the coming of days Joanne and Al really started liking each other more, and more.

They begin to spend lots of time together.

Joanne's mom, and dad begin to allow her more independence by her being a high school student. But she still couldn't have boyfriends. She'd have to lie and tell them that she was going to one of her girlfriend's house, but all along she'd be sneaking around with Al.

They'd do all type of shit together, bowling, skating, going to the show, or museum, joy riding, or just chilling out at his crib.

After a few weeks Al begin trying to get physical with Joanne by trying to kiss, and hug her, she never let him do so.

After a few months passed she still wouldn't let him get physical, it was hard as hell for Al to get the pussy from Joanne.

Al never had to wait that long to get the pussy from no other Ho's in the past.

What really hurt Al the most was that he had put all his other Ho's on the back burner for Joanne, and she wouldn't even let him hug or kiss her after months.

One day Al's house was empty; the entire family had gone to the mall.

Al went to pick up Joanne and took her to his basement which was properly furnished like the rest of the house.

He put a xxx-rated tape in the VCR. She had never even seen an xxx rated movie before.

After a few minutes of watching the movie, the actors, and actress undressed and started fucking.

"What, what, what take me home," Joanne said in a loud rude, manner. "What you uh saying it like that for, if you gone act like that you can walk home for all I give a fuck," he said.

She stormed out of the basement back door, slamming it hard behind herself.

As a few weeks went pass they ignored each other. They would treat each other as they didn't exist.....

Al usually clean's out his locker each Friday to destroy all the scrap paper amongst other things that didn't belong there.

One Friday while Al was cleaning out his locker Joanne accidently bumped into him.

"Damn you just gonna bump into me, and ain't gonna say excuse me," Joanne said.

"Girl you bumped into me," Al said.

As their eyes caught contact with one another, they both begin smiling.

They was happy to see each other, but their foolish pride wouldn't let them show it.

"I'm tired of your shit that's why I kicked you outta my house," Al said in a humorous manner. "I've been kicked out of better places," Joanne said.

"Are you alright do you need a ride home," Al stated.

"No I'm okay I can manage by myself," Joanne said.

"Forgive me for bumping into you," Joanne said. "It's really no big deal, it's always a treat when we meet," Al said.

"I ain't trying to get rid of you, but I gotta finish cleaning out my locker before they close the school for the day," Al said.

"You take it easy, it was good to see you," Al said.

Good to see me, you see me every day in school and don't say shit to me after I didn't wanna fuck, she thought to herself.

"You take it easy to, it was good to see you to," Joanne said, as she began walking away up the hallway.

As she got to the middle of the hallway she turned around and looked back at Al.

"Al, I do need you to drop me off at home my feet are killing me," she said. "A'ight give me a few minutes to finish cleaning out my locker."

As Al and Joanne began on their short ride home they couldn't hide their excitement of being around each other.

"Boy I been missing you," Joanne said. "I been missing you to," Al said.

"I just ain't ready for sex," Joanne said. "I love you, do you love me," Al said. "Yeah I love you," Joanne said. "Well that's what lovers do, make love, "Al said. "I just ain't ready yet," Joanne said. "Well I can't force you to have sex with me, but if we ain't gone be fucking we ain't gone be together," Al said. "I just ain't ready yet," Joanne said.

"From time to time if you need a ride home or someone to talk to it's cool, that's what I'm here for," Al said.

"Hopefully you'll find you a boyfriend that's willing to be with you without sex. If you do, I'm happy for you," Al said.

"Boy why is you driving so slow, you must be high, "Joanne said. "Naw I'm driving slow to enjoy time with you," Al said. "I never seen you drive this slow; you must really want to enjoy some time with me," Joanne said. "Yes, I do, I been missing you," he said.

He pulled on a block around the corner from her house and parked.

"Now get out," he said. "Let's chill here for a little while," she said.

Al smiled, and put a Stevie Wonder 8 track in the radio, Hotter Than July, as they began listening to his song All I Do.

The volume on the radio was at a moderate level; therefore, they could hear the music, and hear each other talk.

"All I do is think of you, to me you're a female guru, that makes dreams come true," Al said.

The poetry made her start giggling.

"You ain't gotta go home, but you gotta get the fuck out my car," Al said. "Why are you in a hurry," She asked? "I got things I need to do," Al said.

"A'ight I'll see you tomorrow at school," she said.

"Tomorrow ain't no school, don't you mean Monday, no Tuesday teachers having a meeting Monday," he said. "Yeah I'll see you Tuesday," she said.

She got outta the car walking slowly to her house, and couldn't stop thinking about Al. Al was a straight player.....

Two days later Sunday afternoon Joanne was at church couldn't seem to take Al off of her mind.

She decided to leave church early because she wanted to go home to call Al and she had a painful headache in which she wanted to take some Aspirins and lay in the privacy of her own bed.

Normally she wasn't allowed to leave church early or leave by herself; but her mom and dad were starting to give her more independence because she was getting older. Besides the walk from church to her home was a short distance.....

As she entered the house she walked passed her sister's bedroom smelled, and even seen smoked. The first thing came to her mind was that something was on fire.

She walked closer to the bedroom; before actually reaching it she became aware that the smoke smelled as Marijuana. She knew the smell very well because Al had smoked Marijuana around her all the time.

Once she walked closer to the bedroom door she noticed that it was open, but only a couple of inches.

She looked in the room and noticed that her sister Roxie and sister's boyfriend Robert was asshole naked performing oral sex on one another at the same damn time.

The first thing came to her mind was to push the door open and say, "I'm telling momma." After a few seconds went by she became pleased with the action.

She noticed how Roxie was putting Robert's entire dick in her mouth as she'd bob her head up and down. She'd start from the top of his dick and go all the way to the bottom with ease.

Being that his dick was about eight inches long and two and a half inches wide. Joanne wondered to herself how could Roxie gobble such mass amount of produce; when I brush my teeth and my tongue I always choke; even when I eat a Banana if I stick it to far in my mouth before biting it I'd choke, Joanne thought to herself.

As they continued oral sexing each other Roxie continued gobbling his dick as Robert's tongue worked her pussy; it was as if it tasted delicious to him.

After approximately ten minutes Roxie took her mouth off his dick and begin saying, "I'm cumming, I'm cumming." Robert then began moving his tongue in and out of her pussy at a swifter pace, as Roxie began

jagging him off.

within seconds Robert released an enormous amount

of nut all in her face, as she was complete cumming.

Next Robert laid Roxie on her stomach and he stuck

his dick in her ass as he began pumping up and down on

her in a stiff and slow rate.

She began crying tears, and hollering, "Roby stop

fucking me in my ass, please stop fucking me in my ass."

Joanne panicked not knowing what to do. Robert

pumped up and down seven times and then nutted.

Afterwards Roxie jumped up and kissed Robert as if he

was just coming home from war or something.....All

along she enjoyed every moment of it. It was like

pleasure and pain all at the same time.

Joanne began to wipe the sweat off of her forehead, relieved from her momentarily sign of distress.

Then Roxie began sucking on his dick for about twenty seconds. She was only sucking it to get it back hard so they could start back fucking.

Now his dick got back hard as a brick, as both of them was standing straight up he grabbed her by her ass cheeks and pulled her close to him and began hugging and kissing her; then he placed his dick gently in her pussy and started fucking her extremely hard to the point where as she was feeling so much pain that she couldn't continue to kiss him, as her hollering got louder.

As Rob proceeded to fuck Roxie, she started to suck on her own titties which was so amazing to Joanne being that she'd never had sex before, let's known seeing others have sex.

Robert and Roxie performed numerous sexual acts for about an hour. Joanne watched and enjoyed the whole session.

Once Roxie and Robert's sexual love was complete, they sat on the bed remaining in the nude, and finished smoking their weed.

They'd puff on the joint two times then pass it to one another, two hits and pass.

After they smoked their weed they got dressed.

Joanne left the house without slamming the front door. She came right back in as if she was just entering it; slamming the door in order to make a loud noise so Roxie, and Rob could hear it to think she was just coming in the house.

Joanne went directly to her sister's room opening the door seeing Rob sitting on the bed. "I'm telling momma that you got a boy in the house while she's not here, give me some money and I won't tell," Joanne said.

Robert and Roxie gave Joanne ten dollars a piece, she was content with the twenty dollars.

After watching Roxie and Robert have sex Joanne was still amazed on how her sister Roxie could gobble his entire dick without choking.

She went into the kitchen and grabbed a Banana out of the refrigerator, placed it gently into her mouth; while the Banana was in her mouth a couple of inches she began to choke, so she took it out. Still clueless on how her sister could devour a dick like that without gagging, or choking.

She went and took a hot shower, while in the shower she began to wash her little pussy, with no hesitation she began fingering herself with one finger from hand with the other hand rubbing her titties. In no time she began cumming now she knew why her sister Roxie kept saying, I'm cumming, I'm cumming, I'm cumming.

The rest of the day, and all that night Joanne couldn't seem to take her mind of Roxie's and Rob's eye appealing sex session.....

It was Monday morning, and it was no school that day; because the teachers at her school was having a meeting.....As Joanne opened her eyes she immediately went into the bathroom to brush her teeth, and wash her face.

After that she ate her breakfast that was prepared for her prior to her mom, and dad going to work. Once she was done eating her bacon, and eggs she decided to get into the tub to bathe. She ran some hot water in the tub filled with bubble bath products, got in the tub rest her body in the hot water and began masturbating once again; the joy and pleasure to her was like a gift, a treasure.

The next day at school Joanne sat in music class smiling at Al, anxiously lusting for him to have his way with her body.

Throughout that entire day in music class, Joanne totally tuned the teacher out. That particular day she wasn't interested in anything but hardcore sex with Al.

As the 6th period music class was over the school bell rang.

"Alright class make sure your homework is on my desk the first thing in the morning," Mrs. Miller said.

Joanne was the first one to leave the class, she wanted to catch Al in the hallway to set a date with him.

As Al came out the class she began smiling imagining his dick going in and out her pussy.

"Hey Al," Joanne said. "Hey what's up Joanne," Al said.

"Can you wait on me after school I need you to drop me off at home," she said. "Yeah I got you, you know I'll do anything for you," Al said.

"A'ight I'll see you then," she said. "A'ight I'll holler at you after school," Al said.

Never in Al's wildest dreams would he have ever imagined that he'd experience the best sex ever with Joanne on that day.

After school Al patiently awaited on Joanne. Once she came out they both entered his car which was parked in front of the school; he immediately played some music by Stevie Wonder titled, Once In My Life. The mood was perfected by the music being at a low tone.....

"Joanne the galaxy's greatest woman whom should be worship by many men; Joanne without you this world shall end, my best friend until the end, Joanne."

To the average individual Al's poetry wasn't shit, but to Joanne she loved it; they made her feel appreciated.

Outta nowhere she asked him could she go over his house to watch some movies, never in his wildest dreams would he have imagined that he was finna get some of that virgin pussy.

Once they went to his house and made their way down the stairs she asked if she could see that sex tape that he played last time, right then and there he knew she wanted to fuck.

He swiftly put the sex tape in.

By her being a virgin, and by him having respect for her he knew he'd have to get her in the mood first before she undressed.

They begin to watch the movie. She became overwhelmed with the action in which turned to lust, in his mind he couldn't wait to tear the pussy up inside her walls nuts he was anxious to bust.

Being indulged in the sight of those two porn stars big ass dicks demolishing this female porn star little ass pussy; this was the best movie she'd ever seen in life.

He sat on her lap and started playing the French kissing game as he'd gently rub her breast. He took off her shirt and bra stopped and gazed at her titties adoring them.

He began sucking her titties nipples as if he was breast feeding himself.

She took off her own pants, panties, shoes, and socks, as he took off all his clothes, both nude as the day they were born.

He laid her down held her legs down by her ear, he had her in a tight lock, because he knew she was a virgin, and wouldn't be able to stand the rain, of pain.

He put the tip in moved in and out a few times just to get her wet the pussy juices instantly began flowing. He started fucking her like he was mad at the world. She repeatedly told him stop Al, stop Al you're hurting me, he didn't listen. In no time she was cumming. He bust a nut in her and got up off her.

She looked at him with a devilish grin upon her face.

She stuck her hand down there rubbed it, come to find out she was slightly bleeding.....

"Boy my stuff bleeding," she said.

He thought she'd be mad cuz he didn't stop when she told him to, but all along she wasn't.

She laid on the bed on her back.

"Let's do it again," she said.

He immediately lifted her legs in the air as he forced his dick in her pussy.

As he began to fuck her hard and fast while listening to her moan he noticed that her titties would bounce differently from the other females he had in the past. They'd bounce as if they had Milk in them or something.

He fucked her for thirty minutes straight. During the entire thirty minutes he noticed that his dick never went soft. Usually with other chicks each time he'd nut his dick would get soft; but it didn't with her simply because her pussy was the best he'd ever had and he'd had many of them.

After they completed fucking they went into the

basement bathroom and prepared bubble

bath to cleanse their body. Once they got into the tub

they took turns bathing each other,

and they took turns fingering Joanne.....

On the way to tour the city, Al blazed up one of the

joints, as they began to drive, they'd look into each

other's eyes as they could see the sunrise. It was if they

were riding off into the sunset.

As Al begin to smoke his weed his mind soared high as

the clouds. Although Joanne didn't smoke none of the

weed it was as she was semi-getting high off the contact

of the potent smoke.

During the ride they listen to Stevie Wonder song

Rocket Love repeatedly. Al had listened to the song so

many times over the years that he knew the song by

hard; he'd repeat this one verse as if he wrote it himself just for Joanne. "I long for you since I was born a woman sensitive and warm, and there you were."

They'd continue to drive through Chicago's downtown area amongst other places.

After a couple hours went past he dropped her off at home.

All that day and all night she fantasized about her and Al's past fuck fest. She felt as she'd worship him for life. For she physically nor mentally had never felt that wonderful.....

Chapter 2

After time progressed along Joanne parents found out that Al, and Joanne was dating. They found out through church members and nosy neighbors who'd see them together on many occasions.

Joanne's parents wanted to attempt to keep them apart but they tried the same thing with some of her older sisters, and their boyfriends and their attempts all were unsuccessful.

Joanne's parents figured they'd allow Joanne to have a boyfriend, but certain rules would apply; she couldn't have Al in the house while they wasn't there. If she was to be in the car with Al or anyone else they must have a

License and Insurance and be a safe driver. As well as he couldn't call the house phone after 9:00 p.m.

Within the year of 1977 Joanne noticed that one month she didn't come on her period. So she knew she was pregnant. She panicked not knowing what to do. She knew that once her family found out she was pregnant she'd have to leave home.

After approximately 2 1/2 months Joanne confessed to Al that she was pregnant; Al was overjoyed. She also explained to him that once her parents found out she was pregnant she'd have to leave home. Al told her to worry about that once that time came.

After approximately 4 1/2 months Joanne pregnancy began showing; her mom and dad immediately told her she had to go, but they'd give her time to find a place to live.

Six months within her pregnancy she found a place within Thurgood Marshall Housing Projects which was approximately twenty minutes away. It was one of the worst places in the city to live; it had a crime rate so high that statistics couldn't account for.

But the rent was cheap and it had free heat, water, and plumbing services. Joanne and Al had it rough financially due to them being so young without very much money.

On July the 18th 1978 the child was born it was a boy.

They named him after his dad, Al. Joanne nicknamed him Lil Al.

When they first brought Lil Al home from the hospital it was wonderful everybody came through bearing gifts, and showing love.

Around the time Lil Al was three Joanne, and Big Al

had a friend name Carlos that got killed, so they

nicknamed Lil Al, Lil Carlos.....

Chapter 3

Al(sr.) begin to utilize Lil Carlos to meet women; Lil Carlos was a handsome little fellow.... One day Al was walking Lil Carlos to their apartment from school. As he entered their apartment building when this older female approached Al, and Lil Carlos. She began complimenting Lil Carlos on his looks.

The old lady walked up to Al and begin shaking his hand. "That's your son, he look just like you," she said.

"Yeah that's my son," Al said. "He so cute," she said. "He take after his dad, you know," Al said, as they both begin laughing.

The old lady went by the name Belinda. She loved having sex with young men. She wasn't interested in a long term relationship, she just wanted hardcore sex.

The young men that she had, had sex with whom lived in the apartment complex nicknamed her Belinda The Blender. She gave sex like she was the one whom made sex up.

"Lil Carlos go push the button for the elevator," Al said.

As Al and Belinda continued to talk Al noticed within her conversation she kept insisting on coming up to their apartment when Joanne wasn't there.

Al knew Belinda wanted to get fucked.

"Yeah come up there in about twenty minutes I need your help filling out some applications," Al said. "Okay I'll be up there twenty minutes on the dot," Belinda said.

"Dad man here go the elevator," Lil Carlos said.

"A'ight I'll see you in twenty minutes, Al said. "Okay I'll be there," Belinda said.

Joanne was at work and Carlos usually go to sleep when he comes home from school, a perfect timing to fuck Belinda.

"Carlos man why don't you go to sleep, and soon as you wake up I'm a take you to McDonald's, Al said.

"Okay dad," Carlos said.

Twenty minutes past and Belinda was knocking on the door. Al opened it and immediately to let her in.

"Hey Belinda come on in."

She entered and sat down on the couch.

"Where the applications at," Belinda asked.

"I can't seem to find them I misplaced them," Al said.

Al immediately converted into a different conversation. As Belinda began to talk, before long Al cut her off, and asked her do she exercise. "I do a little exercise sometime, why did you ask that," she said. "Cuz you got a nice ass to be so old, do you be doing squats," he asked?.....She begin laughing. "I do a little squats."

You have a nice ass, and the rest of your body is shaped as well.

"I've been seeing you around for a long time, and from a far I adore your style, and demeanor," he said.

"It's been a pleasure meeting you," Al said. "Thanks it's been a pleasure meeting you to," she said.

"You look so good to me can I please have a hug," Al asked?

She passionately said, "anytime" as she hugged him tight.

As they hugged he wondered what he would say to get her naked.

She beat him to it, "if you wanna ask me something go ahead and ask," she said.

Instead of him asking he just unbutton her pants took off her pants, and then her panties, and she took off everything else herself.

Minutes later, Lil Carlos was awakening from his sleep. He came into the living room and seen his dad fucking Belinda. This sight was amazing to Lil Carlos.

Carlos vantage point was from the back part of Al and Belinda but he could see them from the side, doing the nasty.

Belinda The Blender was taking all the dick in her pussy like a pro.

She had her eyes slightly open, and seen Lil Carlos as she'd chant Lil Carlos name softly at a low tone. Al was wondering why she was calling Lil Carlos name, but really didn't give a fuck this old lady had a bomb.

Lil Carlos then ran back to his room confused, but yet pleased. All day Lil Carlos contemplated on what he'd seen. He never told no one of the ordeal. But from that day forth Lil Carlos knew that he wanted to forever be a player like his dad.....

Chapter 4

As a few years passed along Lil Carlos found himself getting more in tune and attracted to women.

At times when the guys would be playing sports or doing other things he'd be on the side line fucking with Ho's.

It's as his life would be devoted and dedicated to women.....

Lil Carlos had a cousin whom name was Mike. Mike lived in the same projects, but different building.

Mike was a true player as well; he had natural wavy hair, and talked as a 70's pimp.

In the times when it was cold outside Carlos would have a hood on, and always be mistaking as a girl, he'd hate that.

By the time Carlos was eleven his dad would feed him food for thought as knowledge about fucking with ho's; Carlos would listen to game his dad was giving vividly.

Al starting snorting heroin, and would get drunk off the heroin spilling his guts out to Carlos about player shit.....

"Carlos wake up man it's time to get ready for school," Al said. "Dad man I don't feel like going to school today," Carlos said.

"You gotta go to school, you know your mom gone be tripping if you don't," Al said.

"Gone go to school lil homie, am a pick you up from school, and take you shopping," Al said.

Carlos got up, got dressed and rushed to school.

All day at school Carlos couldn't wait until school was over with, so he could go shopping.

When 2:30 came around Carlos flew outta the school.

Al was parked in front of the school in his white 78 Cadillac, thirties and vogues, gold nose, as L.L. Cool J I Need Love song banged in the trunk and as it was Gorillas in the trunk.

All the kids stood and watched the car in amazement, as if they'd seen UFO, sightings, delighting.

Carlos felt proud to have Al as a dad.

As Carlos entered the car Al turned his music down.

"Dad why you turn the music down," Carlos said. "Cuz the police parked up the street, I don't want them bitches pulling me over on no goofy shit. I don't even feel like being bothered with them right now," Al said.

"I wanted to take you to the mall lil homie, but I'm just gonna take you to Madison, and Pulaski to shop cuz I ain't got time to go all the way to the mall. I got other important shit I need to tend to," Al said.

As they rode a few blocks they got caught at a red light.

Al reached in his pocket pulled out a tiny piece of Aluminum foil, opened it up and snorted all of the dope that was in it.

Carlos was from the ghetto so he been knew his dad was a dope fiend, because he knew signs and symbols of a dope fiend, he closed his eyes, nodding, and scratching. But this was Carlos first time actually seeing his dad snort a bag of dope.

As the light turned green, Carlos told his dad to wake. Al begin cruising and begin kicking it to Carlos about player shit.....

Al seen a Ho walking down the street.

"See ole girl right there," Al said. "Who the old lady dressed up in the business suit dad," Carlos said. "Yeah her," Al said. "Whenever you meet a woman like that, that ain't from the hood, take her to the hood and show her off around the guys and the other Ho's," dad said. "Why dad." "Cuz when the hood niggas and the hood Ho's see her they'll have a different level of respect seeing that you got class and you fuck with raw ass classy Ho's," Al said.

As they continued to cruise to Madison, and Pulaski Al snorted another bag of dope and continued feeding Carlos game.....

"Dad man why your pockets be so fat," Carlos asked?

"That's cuz I always keep a lot of money on me to show off to Ho's, but never let a bitch know how you make your cash flow, and don't give a Ho shit but hard dick and bubble gum, and sometimes act like you fresh outta bubble gum, you feel me son." "Yeah I feel you dad."

"Ho's love being around niggas that's getting money. You'll be surprise on what they will do for it. Money bring out the best in them," Al said.

"Once you get a little older and really start hanging out with ho's make sure to always show them a good time," Al said. "Why dad." "Cuz when you treat them good they be wanna give the pussy up more easily. And when you treat them good they run back and tell their girlfriends, and the women in their family how you been treating them. Before long their girlfriends, and the women in their family is going to wanna fuck with you," Al said.

They pulled up in front of a store on Madison, and Pulaski, Tops and Bottoms.

Al parked and snorted another bag of dope.

"When it comes down to Ho's always remember that once you capture possession of a Ho heart and mind everything she own will become yours, including her body and everything else," Al said.

"Son never forget the number one golden rule to being a player," Al said. "What's that dad?" "Under no circumstances are you to ever trust a ho," Al said.....

Chapter 5

At the age of twelve Lil Carlos and the guys would play a special game with the girls. They'd play catch a girl kiss a girl in the project hallways; sometimes it'll result into a little more than kissing.

One day while playing this game he caught this girl whom went the name of Vanilla. Vanilla really liked Carlos, and little did he know she let him catch her.

As he caught her they immediately begin kissing.

While they were kissing she stuck her hand in his pants and gently begin squeezing his dick. He grabbed her hand; "what the fuck is you doing with your hands down there," Carlos said. "Boy stop moving and give me some of that lil ass dick," Vanilla said. "My dick far from little, I got the worlds biggest dick," Carlos said. "Let me see it than," Vanilla said.

He then stuck his hand in his pants and started to play with it to get it hard to show it off to her. "Damn," she said, thinking to herself this lil motherfucker got a big ass dick.

She began seducing him by placing his hands on her pussy. Then she placed one of her hands on his dick. Then she started back kissing him. He loved every minute of it.

He was a virgin, but on the other hand she wasn't she was a straight freak, straight hood-rat.

He bent her over with the thought in his mind, I'm getting ready to get some pussy.

He tried to place his dick in her pussy and couldn't get it in. He was a virgin and didn't know what he was doing.

For five minutes he continued to try to put his dick in her pussy and couldn't get it in.

Vanilla was experienced and she knew that Carlos was young and in-experienced. She grabbed his dick and put it in her pussy.

After Lil Carlos begin pumping twice the juices and berries in Vanilla's pussy begin flowing.

"Stop boy, stop boy," Vanilla hollered.

Lil Carlos didn't stop he continued tearing her pussy up.

While Carlos continued fucking Vanilla, Carlos cousin Mike came in the hallway and seen them fucking.

Mike went out and told all the other kids of what he'd seen.

After 10 pumps for the first time in life Carlos nutted. To Carlos it felt like his entire body was taking to paradise.

As they both came from the hallway and the kids begin laughing at them because they'd just finish fucking. Carlos, and Vanilla didn't care they wanted to do it again.....

As time progressed along Lil Carlos, and Vanilla became boyfriend and girlfriend.

Lil Carlos cheating on Vanilla from time to time; but Vanilla cheating on him all the time. Although they did cheat neither one never got caught.

Within six months of Vanilla, and Carlos fucking around Vanilla became pregnant.

One day after Carlos had just gave Vanilla the dick in the rawest form she told him she was pregnant. He ask the bitch by who, she told him by you.....

"You momma gone kill us when she find out you pregnant by me," he said. "But we gotta tell your momma, and am a tell my momma," she said.

Carlos got dressed and was on his way out the door. "Where are you going Carlos," she said. "I'm finna go tell my momma," he said. "Call me later on and tell me what you momma said," Vanilla said. "A'ight I got you," Carlos said, as he ran straight out the door.

"Mom," Carlos said? "What boy," Joanne asked? "Guess what," Carlos said.....Carlos stuck his chest out, and said, "I'm finna be a dad." "Who you done got pregnant," she said. "Vanilla," he said. "Vanilla," she said. "That girl ain't pregnant by you," Joanne said. "Yes she is," he said. "Well we gone have to have ya'll take a blood test," Joanne said.

Carlos really didn't wanna take a blood test, he just knew she was pregnant by him.

The days to follow Joanne and Vanilla's mom agreed that Carlos and Vanilla should take a blood test to see if the baby was actually Carlos.

Joanne, Vanilla's momma, Carlos, and Vanilla went to their hood clinic to have the test taking.

The doctor came out like Maury Povich, "Lil Carlos you are not the father," The doctor said.

I knew that lil bitch wasn't pregnant by him, Joanne thought to herself.

Joanne and Carlos begin shaking their heads from side to side, as Vanilla begin crying Joanne and Carlos immediately left the clinic.

On his ride home Carlos begin to visualize in his head his daddy talking to him; son always remember the number one golden rule never trust a woman......

Chapter 6

Carlos daddy Al starting snorting more, and more heroin, eventually fell off and was a straight dope fiend. Al and Joanne had been broke up years prior to him falling totally off. Al ending up moving out of state with some of his family in Mississippi.

Money was kinda tight for Joanne and Carlos although they maintained. Carlos starting hustling selling a little weed for some of the guys in the projects.....

Carlos grandmother lived across the bridge about 15 or 20 minute walk from where he lived. He'd go over his grandmother house and chill from time to time. He pretty much knew majority of the people from the hood, although he grew up across the bridge.

One day he was sitting on his grandma porch chilling, and outta nowhere a cat from the hood named Bo-Diggla just walked up to him, and begin talking to him. He never once had a conversation with Bo-Diggla until then.

Bo-Diggla was a major player on the Ho's, and in charge of two dope operations. Bo-Diggla was a teenager as well, but a few years older than Carlos.....

Bo-Diggla seen Carlos and knew that he wanted to cuff him, and hang out with him because he seen he was player.

In no time flat Bo-Diggla had Carlos hanging with him, and had him running the dope spot.

Bo-Diggla would feed Carlos all the player game, most he had already heard from his dad in his younger days, although some was new to him.

Bo-Diggla and Carlos stayed hanging out together daily, bending on Ho's, and traveling to places Carlos had never been before.....

One day Bo told Carlos they was going to a ballerina show; Carlos laughed and said he not going to no motherfucking ballerina show, but Bo-Diggla convinced him telling him about all the Ho's that would be present.

Once they made it to the place where the play was being held Carlos noticed that the place was smaller than expected. As they begin to enter they noticed everyone there looking all sophisticated within the way they dressed. The auditorium was filled with different races of people.

They sat and watched the show which lasted about an hour and a half to Carlos surprise the show was a bomb.

After the show the performers came off stage to meet the audience.

As Carlos begin shaking the audience hand, this one ballerina caught his eye.

She was pretty as hell. She looked as a European descendant. But in reality she was mixed with black, and white. Her father was black and her mom was white.

Lil Carlos looked into this female ballerina's eyes and it was as he could see a reflection of himself. He noticed two distinguishing features that she possessed that the average white female didn't. She had brown eyes and an enormous ass. When he first looked at her, she looked back at him; from a far it was as they could see eye to eye.

It was the true meaning of love at first sight. As when he walked towards her it was as he was gliding on air. He started speaking to her.....

"Hey, how are you doing? I really enjoyed the show and I would love an anchor presentation, all of the actors played a major role in the success of an outstanding presentation. But your part as a ballerina was the best feature within the play. You deserve a standing ovation. My name is Carlos, and it's a pleasure meeting you, Carlo said. "My name is Katrina, but my family and friends call me Lady Katrina, and my stage name is Ballerina Katrina.....

After hearing her voice he noticed that she had a British accent that sounded so sexy to him.....

"Lady Katrina the world's greatest Ballerina. I'd love a private show," Carlos said as she began to giggle, but gave no answer.

She then noticed from his clothing apparel that he was a street thug. She wasn't really into dating street thugs. But she felt compelled to give Carlos a try because he spoke in a civilized manner in which displayed that he had a little class, also he had a profound vocabulary and clean cut, extremely cute.

"I can give you a private show, here's my telephone number, and address, but call me before you come over to my living quarters," she said.

Carlos face inherited a smile that was as if had been given new life, as if he'd ate from the garden of love, earthly paradise. He immediately wrote down his number on a piece of paper and hand it to her.....

Over a short period of time to overlap Carlos put Katrina as his number one Ho.

Carlos, and Katrina would spend lots of time together. A few times he'd drive her through the hood to show her off because she was showcase material, but she never got out the car.

They'd visit, go to see other plays, art galleries, museums, the zoo, amongst other places.

Even the days when they wasn't together he'd still have long, and meaningful conversations with Katrina over the phone. Her words was like melodies to his ears, wishing he could always have her near.....

After a couple of months went past Carlos begin to get weary of having a relationship with Lady Katrina, because it was difficult to get sex from her. No matter how hard he tried she didn't wanna fuck; it was making him really tired, although he liked her a lot.

As no sex continue to exist Carlos begin to stray away from Katrina; every time she'd call or invite him over he'd make up excuses. Little by little they both begin to stray away from each other until their relationship no longer existed.....

One day Lil Carlos was at the mall shopping by himself. He had approximately $1,100 to shop with. $500 out of the 1,100 was in single dollar bills. So to someone else who's seen the rack of money it looked like much more.

As he was in the dollar store buying hygiene products. As he attempted to pay the cashier this female seen the rack of money, "do you need some help spending that money," she asked, as they both begin laughing.

After he paid for his items, and she paid for hers, they begin to conversate.

Her name was Lisa Ramirez she was half Puerto Rican, and half Mexican.....

As they continue to talk they came to find out they had a lot in common.

They exchanged numbers and went their separate ways.

Four days went pass and Carlos wondered why Lisa never gave him a call. He never called her because he'd always had a notion that if a female was really interested in him she'd call first.

Five days went past Carlos get a call, he asked "who is this." "It's the girl you met at the mall," she replied......I met a lot girls at the mall Carlos thought to himself.

He played it off as he did know who she was, as they talked he could tell by her Spanish accent that it was Lisa.....

She told him that she was just finishing up her homework and decided to give him a call. He instantly started asking questions about her future and what classes she was taking in college. She told him she was studying to get a Master's Degree, as an accounting. The reason she took up accounting is was because she had a fetish for numbers. She went on to tell him her fetish was just like her mom, and dad. Her dad was an economics teacher, and her mom was a math teacher.....

"Enough about me and my family, how are you doing," Lisa asked? "I'm doing good I was just sitting thinking about you, right before you called," Carlos said. "Good game, I don't believe you, if you was sitting thinking of me, why didn't you call," Lisa asked. "I know you probably be busy, so I was just waiting on you to call," Carlos said. "Oh really, good game but I like it."

"You probably just finished riding on some Ho's," Lisa said, as Carlos begin laughing because it was the truth. "I don't consider females to be Ho's, I consider them to be queens," Carlos said.

They talked over the phone for thirty minutes with no end. All the while he wondered if she had a sister for Bo-Diggla.....

"Do you have any sisters, or brothers," Carlos asked? "No I'm a only child," Lisa said. "I'm an only child, as well," Carlos said.

"I have to go I have important business to attend to," Lisa said. "Do you need a ride I can come pick you up, "Carlos said. "No I'm good, I have my own car, but will call you later for sure," she said as both of them said bye then hug up the phone.....

Lisa gave him I call later on; he told her he was in his area and wanted to come through. He bent on her in Bo-Diggla's drop top Corvette, she could smell the weed burning. They kicked it for a little while she was impressed that this young man was pushing a drop top, Corvette.

Once Carlos left Lisa he want to pick up Bo-Diggla, they went to bag up, rock cocaine for both dope operations in which Bo-Diggla was in charge of. They had a team at the table bagging up but it still took many hours to finish.

After they finish bagging up, they sipped a little

champagne while smoking 7 blunts, while riding to a

Pizza place. While at the pizza place Carlos got a call to

his surprise it was Lisa, asking him to come through.....

Carlos immediately rushed over there fantasizing

about serving her pussy raw dick.....

Once he pulled up to her house she ran out titties

bouncing up, and down, pleasing to his eyes.

He begin steaming his marijuana as she could hear the

sizzling sound of the herb being set on fire.....

She asked him to pass it, he couldn't believe it he

didn't even know she smoked.....

Before Carlos knew they were alone in his bedroom

tongue kissing under the moonlight. Carlos upped his

dick on her snatched her shirt and bra off, and began

titty fucking her, in no time he was releasing a load of

nut on her titties. He then snatched her skirt and panties off, and seen a freshly shaved pussy. As he worked his way in with his dick he noticed that the pussy was dry, he worked his dick in and out slowly to get it wet, and in no time flat the pussy was wet. Carlos rammed his dick in and out her pussy in which seems like forever.....

Lisa begin introducing Carlos to some of her friends from school, he hooked them up with Bo-Diggla, Bo-Diggla fucked a lot of her friends.....

Carlos began to notice that one of Lisa's friends Precious liked him. She was mixed Puerto-Rican, and black, a bad bitch.....

Outta nowhere Lisa tells Carlos, "my friend Precious like you." Carlos smiled remained speechless not knowing what to say.....

"She wanna do a threesome with you, and me," Lisa said. He couldn't believe what his ears were hearing as his eyes got buck in amazement. He remained silent for a while at first.....

"When she gone be ready," Carlos asked. "Whenever we ready," Lisa said. "I'm ready know," Carlos said.....

Lisa got on the phone and called Precious to tell her they was ready and on their way.....

Carlos pulled up to Precious house assuming she was on her way out, but she came to the door with nothing on but t-shirts and panties.....

Precious invited them to the bedroom, and immediately undressed, nice small perky titties, hairy pussy, and big round ass.....

Precious didn't smoke, but of course Lisa, and Carlos did. Carlos blazed up the weed, and pulled his pants down to his knees as Precious got on his knees with a aim to please, she started sucking the shit out of his dick. Lisa took her pants all the way off as Carlos passed her the weed Lisa softly told Precious to get over here and eat this pussy and she did just that. As the smoking of weed passing back and forth, Precious took turns performing a bomb on oral sex on Lisa, and Carlos.....they sexed for hours with no break.

This was the girls first time having a threesome, they all loved it......

One day outta no where Lisa, asked the question, "so what do you do for a living, you're a street pharmacist, correct." "No I work at the supermarket," Carlos said. "Do I look like a fool to you," Lisa said. "Naw you look pretty as hell to me," Carlos said as he switched to another subject.....

Carlos knew Lisa was a winner, a collector's item as a keeper. She'd talk to him about everything under the sun, she gave him knowledge about simple things, and great things. She'd even mentioned to him about brushing his teeth to much could, and would mess up his root canal; and about finishing school getting a job with 401k plan, because there was no future as drug dealer......

Bo-Diggla would feed Carlos the player game about dealing with a chick like Lisa. Bo-Diggla will tell Carlos to keep her, and to use but not misuse her for what she was worth. Like for instance if he had a lot of dope money he could use her to clean up his dope money, and if she had good credit he could use her to get cars amongst other things in her name, but to never mess up her credit.....

Lisa would go on to teach Carlos about mortgaging homes, stocks and bonds, and small cap, and large cap investments.

As time progressed along Lil Carlos, and Lisa grew like the planted seed of love to blossom within time.

Lil Carlos ended up getting Lisa pregnant. Lisa's mom, and dad forced her to get an abortion. They didn't believe in females having kids out of wedlock; besides they didn't want her pregnant by some street thug like Carlos. In reality her mom, and dad wanted her to stay away from Carlos. But at the same time she was an adult had to make her own decisions.

Carlos would always cheat on Lisa, but never got caught, Lisa never once cheating on Carlos, she loved him within the essence of time, gracious, and divine.

Chapter 7

In time Carlos was in play to conduct business on both drug operations; mainly his position was to pass out the bundles of rocks to the shift runners, the shift runners would issue the packs out to the pack workers, and Carlos would have to be around both joints to make sure everybody were handling their business appropriately......

The shift runner, shift lasted for 12hrs; even on it's worst days both joints would sell at least 10,000 a shift even when the police was sweating the joints.....

By the joints putting up double digit thousand stacks it's hard to pay attention and focus on the cars coming up the block unless it's a police car.

As the guys on the block yelled, at each and every car

that passed, "rocks park, rocks park, rocks park, an

unmarked car circled the block; in the car was two

planned clothes female officers, the driver nicknamed

was Blondie, she was a black female, she wore blue

contacts, and died her hair blonde that's why they

nicknamed her Blondie.

Blondie was the true essence of a bullshitter. If you'd

seen her walking down the street you'd never imagine a

pretty harmless looking lady such as herself would be a

maniac mentally. Majority of the time when she made

arrest she'd beat up those being arresting, and

occasionally plant drugs.....

She rode up and, her and her partner bailed out on Lil

Carlos, and begin searching him. Although he didn't

possess any illegal products on him he'd still normally

run from the cops, but this time he didn't even get

chance, because Blondie, and her partner bailed out on him to fast from an unmarked car.

As she begin searching him he noticed that she had blemish free smooth skin, and blue eyes, and blonde hair.....

"Are those contacts lenses or your real eyes," Carlos asked.....

She immediately cuffed him up and slapped him, "of course these are contacts lenses, what black person you know got blue eyes," Blondie said.

I know this bitch didn't just slap me, Carlos thought to himself.

After the slap she looked Carlos into his brown eyes it's as she became hypnotize.

"Forgive me for hitting you I've been having a bad day," Blondie said. "I don't give no fuck that don't give you no right to hit me," Carlos said. "Yeah you right," Blondie said.

Blondie's partner started looking at her like she was crazy, he'd never seen her apologize or even be nice to no one, not even her. She was full of rage that none of her co-workers, nor certain family members didn't even like her.

After searching and uncuffing Carlos, Blondie gave Carlos her number and told him to call her and one day she will buy him lunch as a token of her apology. Lil Carlos peeped game, oh she like me, he thought to himself.

As she got in her car and drove off she couldn't cease to imagine kissing Carlos handsome face.

The days to follow she hoped that Carlos would call her.

After the period of seven days Carlos decided to call her; Carlos was still pissed off because she slapped him, and wanted revenge not to slap her back but to take it out on her pussy.

After the call was over the course of a few weeks Blondie, and Carlos begin spending lots of time together.

After a few weeks Carlos, and Blondie begin fucking on a daily basis.

Blondie went and purchased lots of lingerie sets in which she'd like to wear for Carlos.

Blondie loved rough sex, and Carlos didn't mind giving it to her.

A few times they'd roleplay; Carlos would dress up like the cop, and she'd be the robber. He'd handcuff her imitate as if he was a bad cop forcing her to have sex.

Sometimes when they'd roleplay Carlos would act like he was a rapist forcing her to have sex, by raping her in the ass. She liked getting fucked in the ass.

Blondie became his number one. Lisa was his number two, when he wasn't with Blondie he'd be with Lisa. Because of Blondie, and Lisa his other Ho's would get less time, but he still found a little time to fuck with his other Ho's.

Before long Blondie begin taking drugs from other dope dealers and giving them to Carlos to sell to make a profit for him and her. She was eventually stationed in a high crime area where this Latino gang dwelled named the Latin Kings. Her captain assigned her to this area because it was lots of drug selling and gang banging in this area. He knew she could help downgrade crime in that area. The only drugs the Latin Kings sold was Marijuana, and PCP. They didn't believe in selling any other drugs or using any other drugs besides Marijuana, and PCP. they felt any other drug was an abomination to mankind. Which was ironic cause PCP is one of the most dangerous drug that ever existed.

Blondie would make up fraudulent search warrants and raid the houses in which the Latin Kings stored pounds of Marijuana and PCP. She'd let them keep the PCP, her and some of her crooked officers would split the pounds of Marijuana and the money and wouldn't make any arrest.

Lil Carlos continued to run the other two operations, and manage his own weed spot which was right up the block from one of the spots in the hood. Bo-Diggla was proud that Lil Carlos had opened up his own weed spot. Lil Carlos never told no one where he was getting the pounds from. Nor did he even mention to Bo-Diggla that he had a police officer as one of his girlfriends.

Chapter 8

Lil Carlos would find himself getting into many

unexpected fuck fest with women.....one day he met

this chick named Red. Red was pretty as hell, a red bone

with natural brown hair, and hazel brown cat eyes, she

was petite, nice little titties, nice little ass.

Red was one of the guys from the hood main-

girlfriend. He met Red through buying pounds of weed

from her main-boyfriend Ant. When Blondie couldn't

take weed from the Latin Kings he had to buy pounds

from Ant at $600 a piece just to keep his joint flowing.

Ant had a convenient store in the hood. Ant use the

store as a way for people such as Carlos to buy pounds

of weed without looking suspicious.

Coincidently each time Carlos would purchase weed

from Ant Red would be there. Red would see Carlos and

liked his style and appearance. Sometimes he'd even

crack a few jokes just to past time, she liked that he'd

always put a smile on her face. He had no intentions on

getting with Red but little did he know she wanted him.

One night all of Carlos pack workers whom sold his

weed for him went to a concert, therefore he was

forced to sell his own weed packs. Red came up

attempting to purchase two dime bags of weed. While

she was purchasing the sacks of weed Lil Carlos begin to

inquire of Ant's whereabouts. Lil Carlos wanted to

purchase some pounds. In her own mind she

automatically assumed that he was asking about Ant

only phony kicking it because he actually wanted to

creep off and have sex with her, her assumptions was

wrong.....

He asked her if she'd be seeing Ant tonight. "I ain't gone see him tonight, I ain't gone see him tonight, I ain't gone see home tonight," Red kept saying.

Carlos wasn't paying attention that she was saying she wasn't going to see him tonight several times given him the green light that if he'd want to they could creep off tonight.....

After she'd purchased she slowly walked to her car which was within close distance looking back at Carlos as if she was anxious for him to say something that would brighten her night.....

She drove off slowly and came right back around the block told him to hurry up, and get it in the police was doing sweeps. With no hesitation he got in the car with her as they rode off under the moonlight destination unknown.

As they hit the e-way, Carlos begin to think to himself, since when do they do sweeps at night, sweeps are always during the day.....

They drove the city streets for an hour all the while Carlos hoped and wish nobody had stolen his weed pack in which he left on the joint when Red picked him up.....

After an hour Red pulled up to a Motel now everything all added up to Carlos, it was all a scheme Red wanted to fuck.

Once they got into the Motel room Carlos immediately undressed, then Red undressed. She laid on the bed flat on her stomach. She liked getting hit from the back one way or the other. He climbed on top of her with joy as his dick begin devouring the walls of her Vagina. Now he knew why Ant was in love with Red the pussy was superb.

He adored how that yellow bone's booty bounced in the midst of sex.

After sexing for a long time they both laid on the bed naked as the day of birth, appreciating great sex for what it was worth.

They set flaming fire to the blunt inhale, exhaling loving the stimulation, the smell.

As it was Carlos turn to smoke, Red gently grabbed his dick, and put her face down there, "Damn your dick big as hell you must be retarded or something," Red said.

As she sat and examined it close up a light bulb came over Carlos head she must want to suck it, he thought to himself.

Outta nowhere Carlos told her gone suck it. She paused and looked at him crazy, but then she went on and started sucking it, her mouth was fantastic, in return he ate her pussy to him it tasted great.

Overtime Carlos, and Red continued to creep, and was never caught. Carlos was the first one that introduced her to wearing thongs, her booty looked great in thongs.....

Ant had lots of pounds, on several occasions Red would steal pounds from Ant to give to Carlos. Ant had so many pounds he never knew that they were missing.

After several months Ant and Red broke up because Ant was into domestic violence, and had lots of other Ho's he cheated with, and wasn't a good father to the kids.

Carlos put Red on his team made her one of his main Ho's. But he told Red she must never let Ant find out they were lovers, because it might interfere with their business venture of him buying pounds from Ant, as needed. She understood and respected his wishes. She even told Carlos of some of the apartments Ant had up north where he stored his drugs at; therefore if he wanted to rob Ant he could do so. Her given him this information came to no surprise to Carlos his dad had taught him at an early age to never trust a Ho. After that day he made sure never to let Red know where he was holding his drugs at.....

One night Lil Carlos and Bo-Diggla went to an R. Kelly concert in an exclusive club downtown. They had a nice time at the concert.

After leaving the concert Bo-Diggla begin contemplating on how Carlos had been lacking on hustling in the streets.....

"Man lil homie you been bullshitting on standing on the business," Bo said. "What do you mean by that,"

Carlos asked? "You ain't been standing on my joints like you use to, and you only been keeping your weed spot open for 12hrs a day, keep your weed spot open 24hrs a day the more it's open the more money you receive. You been to busy focusing on Ho's. Ho's come and go you can always bump a Ho," Bo-Diggla said.

Carlos paused remaining speechless.....

"You spend money foolishly man, you got more coats than me, you got about 10 Pelle's that's too much bro. It's cool to spend money from time to time to enjoy yourself, but you need to save more money for a rainy day, you need to save money to bound out and to invest into some things that will make you more money," Bo-Diggla said.

Bo-Diggla dropped Carlos off and they went their separate ways.....

Twenty minutes later Carlos car was totaled by a hit and run drunk driver. Bo-Diggla's uncle had a tow truck business, Carlos called him to come tow is car. Carlos took out the sounds amongst other things that was still useful.....

Bo-Diggla came to pick Carlos up from his uncle shop.....

"I need me a new car, Imma have to hustle hard this week to make some money to buy one," Carlos said. "See I told you, you gotta have money stack for a rainy day," Bo-Diggla said.

"Can I keep one of your cars," Carlos asked Bo. "Hell yeah, no problem, but you gotta start stacking for a rainy day, I'll buy you a car in the morning," Bo-Diggla said.

Bo-Diggla dropped Carlos off in the projects to Carlos mom house. Carlos went straight in as his mom had food ready, he ate smoked a blunt and went back to sleep.

The next morning as the sunlight of day shined across his face, memories of himself as a kid to play came across his mind in such a way.....

He immediately called Lisa to tell her what had happen. She was glad that it was no injuries, and told him that in the future he should get car insurance so that if anything should happen to his car the insurance company would pay him for damages.

Lisa and Carlos talked for a while, even had phone sex, as Lisa fingered her pussy imagining Carlos dick going in and out her pussy.....

Once they finished talking on the phone, Carlos

smoked a blunt and laid out on the bed dick hard as a

brick thinking of pounding away at Lisa's pussy as he fell

into a deep sleep.....

Chapter 9

As he was walking through the park from his mother's apartment going where his homies hung out at, and where Bo-Diggla's and his own dope spot was, he came across a female name Nikki whom he had known almost his entire life. To him she was simply one out of hundreds of females he knew from the hood. Nikki was the type of female that was interested in one thing from men and that was money. As he walked past her he said hi, she said hi back, and they both kept stepping.

As Lil Carlos got approximately 30 feet away she called his name. "A Carlos, are you coming to Big Tricey's party tonight." He looked back at her. "Yes," he said as he turned around and kept stepping. Not knowing that she was inviting him to her vagina, and to Big Tricey's party.

Once he made it to Bo-Diggla's drug spot he went to the house where, Bo-Diggla stored bundles of drugs at.

He took bundles of drugs and took it to the workers. He then went to the house where he stored his weed packs to give to his workers to sell on his weed joint.

As the day progressed along Carlos had a good day. No one on either joint his or Bo-Diggla's spot was arrested nor robbed.

After a hard day of hustling in the streets he went to his mom's apartment to change clothes. While in the process of changing clothes he attempted to figure out which female he'd fuck this particular night. Then he remembered that Big Tricey was having a party this night. Not only was Big Tricey party's live, but it would be tons of Ho's there.

Once he made it to Big Tricey's party he noticed that it was over 500 people there. Players from everywhere, was there. And where's there's players there's Ho's. It was like a car show, and fashion show mixed. The scenery was marvelous as the moonlight, and street lights lite up the nights, as clouds of weed smoke brought forth a delight.

After ten minutes of partying Nikki seen Carlos fixing him something to eat, and begin leaning all on him as if they were lovers. All night Carlos couldn't shake Nikki she really wanted him.

As the night grew old Nikki asked Lil Carlos for a ride home, she lived in the exact same apartment complex as his mom Joanne. He told her he didn't have a car at this point in time. Nikki asked him to walk her home. This seemed strange to him because it was over 500 people at this party, and over half of them had cars; therefore he thought to himself why she want me to walk her home, but he did anyway outta the kindness of his heart.

Her apartment complex was twenty minutes away. As they walked, and talked she begin telling him about all her secrets, and ex-lovers. He began to wonder why is she telling me these things. Also during the walk to her apartment they smoked two blunts. She told him that she didn't have a boyfriend and that her kids were at there grandmother's house.

Once they made it to there apartment complex, he attempted to go his separate way to his mother's apartment as she was suppose to go to her own apartment. She then asked him if he could walk her to her apartment because the hallways was dark and she felt safe with him walking her to her apartment.

Carlos was a player so of course he walked her to her apartment.

Once he walked her to her front door, she insisted that he come in to finish smoking the rest of the weed, he agreed.

Once he got into the apartment he immediately noticed that the apartment was clean as hell. She went into the bathroom as he sat on the couch to relax.

While she were in the bathroom she hollered out the door, "If you want something to drink look in the refrigerator and get you whatever you want out of it, make yourself at home." He looked in the refrigerator and noticed that the inside of it was extremely neat, and well organized like the refrigerators on TV commercials. Although she lived in the projects her apartment was decent.

He grabbed a beer and sat back on the couch.

After a few minutes she came out with a T-shirt on with no pants or shorts on. Never in his wildest dream would he believe that she wasn't wearing panties or a bra under it. When she came out with the T-shirt on he simply figured she was just getting comfortable in her own apartment, but that wasn't the case, she wanted to fuck.

As they blazed the weed, and begin smoking, she sat across from him with her legs wide open, and that's when he noticed that she didn't have on any panties. Her pussy had more hair than a mini afro.

Now it came to reality to Carlos that Nikki was interested in making him, happy within sex. Spontaneously he got on his knees and looked directly between her legs; she looked at him with a devilish grin because this is what she'd wanted.

He immediately removed her shirt from her body. She had some of the biggest prettiest titties he'd ever seen in life. In addition her skin was smooth as a baby.

Usually when Carlos fucked women that had kids they would possess stretch marks, primarily on their stomach; he was amazed that she didn't have any stretch marks on her.

As he proceeded to remove his own clothes in a matter of seconds he fucked her right then and there on the couch.

She was in a counterclockwise position as he thrust his dick in and out her pussy repeatedly; during the process he kept his eyes on the prize, that pussy.

He adored watching the intimate pleasure of his dick going in and out her pussy.

To him it was the greatest show on Earth.

As intercourse continued he noticed that Nikki had an enormous smile upon her face.

He had sex with women more times than he could count or even remember but he'd never put a smile on a females face during sex.

After Nikki, and Lil Carlos was complete sexing. Unexpectedly to Carlos surprise Nikki put her face within his lap and begin sucking his dick. Her oral sex was amazing to him.

Majority of the females would make him cleanse his genitals thoroughly before oral sex; not her she sucked dick straight out the pussy, and did it like a pro. She successfully utilized a method of slow motion. She would move her head up and down, it was as she was trying to swallow his entire dick as if she was attempting to suck the nectar out of it. While she was performing oral sex on him he noticed that she had her legs wide open playing with her own pussy with her fingers. He looked closer to her playing with her own pussy and became aware that she was rubbing the outer layers of it gently in a circular motion; after approximately a minute he noticed that the juices begin slightly shooting out of the hole of her pussy. The sight looked so good to Lil Carlos.

Once he was on the verge of releasing his nut he grabbed the back of her head and begin pumping his dick in her mouth while choking her with his dick, she liked it. When he let his nut go in her mouth she got up and grabbed his hand and led him to her bedroom. She wanted to show off her bedroom set which consist of a Tommy Hilfiger pillowcase and sheets on the bed. The paintings on the wall was of a bootleg Mona Lisa, 2Pac, and Malcolm X. The floor was white and so clean that it shined like it was Marble; the floor was clean enough to eat off of.

She stood against the wall and told him to come closer, as he came closer she grabbed some K-Y jelly from the top of her dresser. She began lubricating his dick herself, and jagging him off at the same time, with hopes of getting his dick hard as a brick. Once it was hard she turned around and she placed it in her ass-hole. Again this wasn't normal because the average female couldn't endure the pain of getting butt-fucked.

He began butt-fucking her with long, hard, and slow strokes to inherit great stimulation. They both enjoyed themselves.

After he nutted she turned around and hugged him. She was a few inches taller than he was. By her being the tallest and being in custody of those gigantic breast she sat her breast on his chest partially covering his face as she was trying to dominate him. Covering her breast on men was something she loved doing; to her it was a sign of power she felt as the queen of all queens.

She hugged him around his neck and he inserted his dick in her pussy, and then hugged her under her arms, and around her back palming her ass. As he began fucking her fast and hard her titties remained covering his chest and part of his face; to him and her the sex was great.

While still in the midst of sex she started moaning in his ears. As she'd moan she'd repeatedly say, "I love you, I love you, I love you."

They smoked weed and fucked all night on and off.

She told Carlos that she had been secretly liking him for many, many years.

She told him she never did a threesome, but she wanted to do one with him.....

Later on in life they began to do threesomes with other women, but never got in a relationship just remained fuck buddies.

Chapter 10

After a few days of hustling Carlos had only made a few thousands. He wanted to buy a car that was more expensive than a few G's. He decided to stay in the house one day, because he didn't want to be on the joints to many days at a time because he'd be to hot with the police. Crooked cops would see drug dealers standing on corners repeatedly and would plant drugs on them if they couldn't catch them with none.

On this day he decided to stay in the house and chill out. His cousin Jackie and her friend Tasha was there.

Tasha was only visiting, Jackie lived there because her mom Diane, Joanne's sister was a crackhead and really didn't give a fuck about Jackie, she was more interested in crack. At this time Jackie was a teenager but carried herself as an adult.

Carlos went into his mom's apartment and took a brief nap.....Once he awoke from the nap he went into the bathroom brushed his teeth and blazed up a blunt.

While Carlos was getting high he begin cracking jokes and basically being himself. Carlos had an out-going personality that women adored. After cracking a few jokes and putting a smile on Jackie's and Tasha's face, Carlos went to one of the back bedroom's to relax. The bedroom door was closed, Jackie came knocking on the door. Once he opened it she told him that Tasha liked him, and she wanted to start fucking with him. "A'ight that's cool," Carlos said half heartedly.

Thirty minutes later Jackie came back knocking on the door saying Tasha said what's up. Carlos half heartedly told her to tell Tasha to come back here.

Once she came into the room Carlos locked the door put on an xxx-rated tape in the VCR, and commence to smoking his Marijuana, he offered Tasha some she didn't accept it she didn't smoke.

Tasha was cute but a little chubby. Carlos was never interested in her but he was high, and wasn't going to pass up the opportunity on getting his dick wet.

Tasha eyes begin to get big mesmerized by the action on the xxx-rated tape.

Outta nowhere Carlos just told Tasha to take her clothes off. To his surprise she did it with no hesitation. Tasha felt that any individual she had sex with would be a potential boyfriend, she wasn't up with just simply creeping off, therefore she had no problem with giving up the pussy on the first date if she felt a man would qualify to be her boyfriend.

Once she got undressed Carlos slipped his boxers and t-shirt off.

As she laid on her back, he held her legs in the air on the verge of sticking his dick in her pussy. He paused for a few seconds wondering if he should use a condom or not; Bo-Diggla had been whispering in his ear about safe sex, and he'd frequently be seeing safe sex/H.I.V. commercials.

He decided to run in her raw because she was young and it was unlikely that she had H.I.V. or any other disease. What he didn't know was that H.I.V. or any other disease didn't discriminate off age.

Carlos was high as kite dick hard as a brick he slid raw dick in her. Once entered he seen that the pussy was already super wet, I thought the pussy would be wet and garbage. Oh how he was wrong after a few pumps he begin talking to himself damn this pussy, damn pussy good, damn this pussy a bomb. She made wonderful sound effects, "Uwwww, sssss, uwwww, sssss, uwwww, ssss," as they exchanged fuck faces.

In no time he was the verge of nutting he contemplated on should nut in her or pull it out, he definitely didn't want to get her pregnant. The pussy was so good that he decided to go ahead and nut in her......

Carlos had, had sex with many women before, but Tasha had the best pussy he ever had in life.

The next morning Carlos gave Tasha the nickname of Lady Vagina, he had got that name off a James Bond movie.

Tasha had told Carlos she been liking him for years. Carlos asked her why she never said anything. Tasha told him girls just don't do that, they don't try to get with guys they wait on a guy to get with them.

Carlos fucked Tasha a few more times after that night; he stop fucking with her after those few fucks because she wanted a boyfriend, and Carlos wasn't interested in being her boyfriend.

Carlos didn't miss her at all, but Carlos did miss the pussy.

Chapter 11

After weeks of hard hustling Lil Carlos saved up

enough money to purchase a car he desired. Bo-Diggla

would've brought him or car or even would've helped

him get a car, but he decided to do it on his own. He

brought him a newer model four door Cutlass. He took

Lisa's advice on how to convince the sales person to

charge him the invoice price for the car, and it worked.

He took the sounds that he had in his car that he had

the accident in and put them in the Cutlass. He liked his

new car better than the old one.

With his new car he felt as a kid again when his

mother would tell him to stop showing out in front of

company.

Once he got his sounds installed he went straight to

the hood to show out.

He went through the hood with his sounds turned up

beating up the block, as weed smoke flowed freely out

of the sun roof.

The same day his mom Joanne needed to use the car

to go to work. Lil Carlos was like I'll drop you off and

pick you up. Joanne said no I need to keep the car, because I need to do some deliveries, she worked for a flower shop.

Lil Carlos agreed to let her keep the car as much as he really didn't want to because it was his first day having it. He wanted to enjoy himself. But he knew she needed it to do her job at work.

Also, that her job was more important than him joyriding. He gave her the car stayed in the house enjoying phone sex with Lisa.

As hours progressed along Joanne came to the apartment for her lunch break. She didn't usually come all the way back to the apartment for a lunch break she'd usually stop at a fast food joint.

Once Joanne made it within their apartment she came in the door with a female friend/co-worker. Joanne told

Carlos that her friend Cookie was having problems with this warrant, but it was only for traffic, that she had wanted to get it squashed; Cookie was worried that if she didn't get it squash she'd have to serve time in prison.

Carlos mention to Cookie the proper steps to get the warrant squash and expunged from her record. As well as she must get a new court date and that this time she must be present in court.

Carlos noticed that Cookie kept talking to him about the warrant after he already vividly explained to her the situation.

She began asking dumb questions, Carlos wasn't aware that she was asking dumb questions because she liked him and simply just wanted to continue their conversation.

It was time for Cookie and Joanne to go back to work, but Cookie act if she was sick with a stomach ache, but all along she wasn't.

Cookie pleaded with Joanne to stay at her apartment, at least until later on. Joanne agreed because Cookie was a good friend and a great co-worker, and Carlos would be there.

Joanne left Carlos went into the backroom and started watching the news. Cookie came to the back asking dumb questions, outta nowhere Cookie asked Carlos, "would you fuck me." Carlos couldn't believe his ears. "What you say," Carlos asked. "Would you fuck me," Cookie said again.

With no hesitation Joanne and Carlos undressed he then told her to suck it first, she did so. She began sucking his dick as he grabbed her by the back of her head with his hand and begin guided her head back and forth as he'd commence to feeding her the dick.

Then he laid her on her back he immediately noticed the cut on her stomach and how hairy her pussy was. What he didn't know was that the cut on her stomach was because they had to cut her open through child birth.

She held her legs up as Carlos eagerly put the condom on his dick, hungry, starving for the pussy.

After they fucked and sucked for a slight moment within time. They smoked the last of Carlos Marijuana. Cookie pulled out a Phillie blunt emptied the tobacco and filled the blunt with weed, rolled it up, let it dry for a few minutes, and then set a blazing fire to it.

Once she passed it to Carlos he could immediately tell that the shit was a bomb it tasted wonderful as he inhaled, and exhaled the potent smoke.....

Cookie's entire plan was to get Carlos high and sex him up. Oh how her planned worked.

Once they completed smoking the weed she laid on the bed holding her legs in the air and put two of her fingers on the outta layer of her pussy opening it up craving for more of Lil Carlos dick. Once Carlos entered he tore the pussy up, at the same time he began tongue kissing and switching up to sucking on her titties one by one as he continued tearing the pussy up.

They took a pause blazed up more Marijuana both with mean mugs on their face as if they were getting ready to fight within a boxers or wrestling match.

As they started back fucking Cookie would talk to him while they were fucking.....

"You're doing a great job, keep up the good work, I'm proud of you, you're gonna get an A in sex education," Cookie said.

As she was a pro within sex she could basically tell when a man was on the verge of releasing. As he was getting ready to nut he begin to fuck her faster and harder before he could release she told him to release in her face, and he did so willingly.

She was pleased to see the large amount of nut. To her large amounts of nut meant that her pussy, and seductive talk was at it's best.

She turned over and laid flat on her stomach and looked at him and smiled as she had just won the Lottery jackpot of a million dollars. He looked at her ass as if it was a symbol of greatness. He climbed on top of her, laid flat on her and begin fucking her fast and hard. She adored every second of it. She began talking to him and moaning at the same time.

"Yes baby fuck me like that, it's wonderful, keep up the excellent work your dick feels great," Cookie said.

Carlos was mesmerized by the way her butt cheeks would bounce up and down. At this very moment he felt like he was in paradise.

As they continued fucking as he begun to release, he took it out put it in her mouth. She began sucking his dick as she was a baby attempting to get milk out of it. Once it came out his dick she swallowed all of his love juice, with her nasty ass.....

Chapter 12

Lil Carlos always found himself getting into surprise fuck fest with females. Approximately one week after his sex fest with Cookie he was walking through the hood one day after he'd took his car to the car wash in the hood, Charlie C's.

On his way walking to the joint for business reasons and to hang out and kick it, he seen some chick sitting in a car, he glanced at her out the corner of his eye wondering if she was an undercover or not. As he passed her car she called him to the car and asked him did he know where she could get some weed from, he told her he normally sell weed but his joint ain't been working for a few days his normal connects had been out so he ain't been working.....why did I tell this bitch all that information, that was dumb I should've just told her where another weed spot was at he thought to himself.....

"They got some lime green on Central Park, and Lexington right at the very corner," he said. "Yeah I know where Central Park, and Lexington is at can you get in and go with me," she asked? With no hesitation he jumped in, as they made their way to the weed spot.

Once they made it to the weed spot he brought a bag, she brought a bag. They went and got blunts and some wine coolers, the wine coolers was for her.

They rode the town inhaling, exhaling stimulating their minds, windows rolled up as clouds of smoke was all that could be seen passing through time.....

Once they finished smoking, and drinking she dropped him off at his car as they exchanged numbers and went separate ways.

After that day he kicked it with her several more times smoking, and drinking but no sex, she wouldn't give the pussy up.

On the fourth time they kicked it once they finished smoking and drinking Carlos told her to drop him off. As they drove to the drop off destination she begin telling him that she needed sex, she hadn't been fucked in months because her boyfriend was in jail. Carlos knew what time it was.

They ended up at Carlos mom's house. When they first got there she acted if she was scared to go into the projects; but he convinced her to go in.

They made it to the apartment, and went to the back room and got naked. She wasn't the cutest thing but naked she beautiful.

Once she got undress the funky aroma that her pussy upheld instantly lingered in the room, smelled like death.

Carlos held his nose bent her over put on the rubber and tore the pussy up. Immediately afterwards Carlos got dressed made her get dressed lied and told her he had to go take care of some business, after that time he never kicked it with her again. Every time she wanted to kick it he'd make up an excuse why he couldn't. But in reality the pussy smelled to horrible for him to want to do it again.

One day walking through the hood outta nowhere a female approached him to strike up a conversation. Her name was Tabatha, she had brown skin with natural curly hair with a body that made men fantasize, she wore glasses and talked professional as if she was a college professor. Carlos automatically assumed he had a winner. All along she was a straight hoodrat, bustdown.

Carlos and Tabatha talked for a brief moment within time; Carlos came to find she was 26 with no kids, he really thought he had a winner. Come to find out she smoked weed. Carlos got into the car with her as they drove to weed spot, Carlos couldn't wait to find a connect with good weed because he knew he was missing out on plenty money.

As they made it to the weed spot he approached the individual that was serving the weed he seen two of his homies, Rob, and John. Rob, and John was like I see you're chilling with Tabatha. "Where do you know her from," Carlos asked them? "That Ho ain't on shit me and John bust that Ho down last night," Rob said.

"Damn she getting down like that," Carlos said. "Hell

yeah, when I first met the Ho, I thought she was a

winner, she ain't on shit. You can take her in the alley

and fuck her right now," Rob said. "For real," Lil Carlos

said.

Lil Carlos ran back to the car overjoyed knowing he

was getting ready to fuck. By him being a player he'd

never tell Tabatha what the guys had told him.

As they rode under the Moonlight he told her to stop

at the liquor store. He went in to get some blunts and

cheap Champagne, Andre extra dry.

Once he came out the liquor store he asked her if she

wanted to get a room. She told him that they didn't

have to get a Motel room. He automatically assumed

she was bullshitting all along she wasn't she was

indirectly letting him know that they didn't have to get a

room they could fuck in the car. He convinced her to get

a room.

Once they got in the room he turned to the xxx-rated

channel, she told him to turn she didn't want to watch

that kind of movie; once again he assumed she was

bullshitting.

After smoking half the blunt he remembered what rob

told him, he straight forward asked her to take her

clothes off she did it with no hesitation.

Once she got undressed he noticed that she had

tattoos on her titties and ass cheeks. The tattoo on her

titty was a red rose. The tattoo on her ass was a tattoo

of a man and woman having sex. As she undressed she

smiled amazed and pleased by the enormous size of his

dick. She laid on her back then he took a condom outta

his pants pocket which was on the floor, placed the

condom on, put her legs on his shoulder inserted his

dick in her and commence to fucking. As he began

fucking her he became shock on how tight her pussy

was. Usually when a female is a big bust-down her

pussy normally is big because of all the dicks that in and

out of it. In the process of him hitting that shit Tabatha

facial expression looked as she was feeling the best

pleasure she'd ever felt in life. As he began to release

his nut he took it out snatched the rubber off and let

lose on the tattoo on her titty. Lil Carlos was the true

definition of a freak.

He put on another rubber and stood her up bent her

over and begin hitting her from the back, she loved it.

Once he released his nut in the pussy he then fucked

her in the ass. For hours they fucked. He wanted to

spend a night with her but she was in a deep

relationship with someone else and couldn't just simply

spend a night out without her boyfriend not knowing of

her whereabouts. As they finished their fuck session Lil Carlos noticed that she immediately went to brush her teeth and shower. After seeing that he knew she was clean. A lot of Ho's he'd fuck, they'd just fuck and wouldn't even cleanse themselves afterwards. Then and there he knew he'd fuck her again. Once she drooped him off in the hood they exchanged numbers. She told him you can't call my house cuz I live with my fiancée, his eyes opened with amazement. He was like damn you're engaged to be married. She then explained to him that her fiancée was a good man. He began thinking to himself like damn you engaged and I fucked you without even spending time with you or convincing you to fuck.

Once again Carlos remembered the golden rule that dad taught him, never trust a Ho. Carlos was like damn it's gonna be hard for me to get engaged, married, or faithfully committed to any Ho.

As weeks progressed along Carlos and some of his homies was riding around chilling. He got a call from Tabatha she wanted to kick it and fuck again, Carlos told her he was chilling with some of his homies and didn't want to drop them off. Tabatha told him you can bring them with us. Then Carlos remembered that Rob said she was a bustdown. He told his homies that she wanted to get bust down. Of course his homies was all for it. They went and got a camcorder. They took her to an expensive Hotel and gotta Jacuzzi sweet. One of his homies Chon brought some pills to the Hotel. Once they got to the Hotel Chon told everybody to take a pill. Everybody took a pill. The pill was X, he wanted everybody sex drive to be at it's all time high.

As one man fucked her from the back she sucked one of the other ones dick, she loved being treated as a slut. They'd take turns fucking her and getting their dick suck. One guy came with a bright idea he stuck his dick in her ass, as another guy had his dick in her pussy while she sucked the other one's dick. It was always one of them on the side recording the entire ordeal. They even gave her a golden shower pissed on her.

Carlos enjoyed himself but yet and still wondered how could a Ho like this be engaged to be married. She wanted to leave after a few hours, but the guys held her hostage for the entire day.

After that night Carlos and his homies fucked her a few more times. They ended up selling the sex tapes in the hood for $20 they made a nice profit of selling hundreds of tapes in the hood.

Chapter 13

Lil Carlos always found himself getting into close love

affairs with the neighborhood rats. One of his favorite

hoodrat was Tina. He nicknamed her Misdemeanor Tina

because she stayed in the police station for being arrested for crimes lesser than felonies.

Carlos knew Tina since he was a little boy. Tina was a few years older than him. At this time both of them was adults. Every time Tina would see Carlos she'd be all over him like they were lovers even before they actually became lovers. Lil Carlos and Tina enjoyed going clubbin. They would always end up at the same clubs by coincidence.

Lil Carlos assumed that Tina was being cool with him simply because they grew up together and she liked him as a friend. Oh how he was very, very wrong. Tina wanted Lil Carlos as her boyfriend.

One day at a club which was a short period away from the hood, Tina was all over Lil Carlos like never before. She began complimenting him about his looks, his outfit, and his personality. As he was sitting on the bar she sat directly on his lap and stated, would you buy me a drink. Now it all came to light to Carlos, she like him, and wanted to fuck. He brought her several drinks.

After the party that night she offered to give Lil Carlos a ride, he told her no he had his own car. She then asked him can I go with you, he said hell yeah.

They ended up at a sleazy motel room. Before long they both was nude as she rode his dick, like the rodeo show. During the entire ordeal of sex she was the dominant one.

Tina stood tall over him. She enjoyed dominanting him within sex.

He turned her over and begin hitting it from the back.

"You can't hit this shit no harder than that, nigga you hit like a bitch," Tina said, as Carlos begin fucking her harder.

That made the sex even more intense because of the way she began talking dirty to him. He begin talking dirty back to her.

"You big fat bitch maybe if your pussy wasn't so big I wouldn't have to hit it harder," Carlos said.

She liked it when men talked dirty to her within sex.

Carlos began slapping on her ass cheeks and fucking her harder than ever, to her this was a blessing.

He continued to talk dirty to her.

"You fat ass bitch you should've douche your pussy, your pussy stank," Carlos said.

After fucking, Lil Carlos was amazed that he fucked Tina so easy, because everyone Tina had given sex to paid lots of money.

Once they was done fucking Tina got smart at the mouth.

"You ain't on shit, you don't know how to fuck," Tina said as they immediately begin laughing.

They sat back and sparked up a blunt filled with weed. Blowing clouds of smoke out their nose, and mouth.

"It took you little ass all this time to figure out I liked you," Tina said.

"I assumed that you was only being friendly," Carlos said.

"Friendly, every time I see you I'm all on you showing you love," Tina said.

Carlos couldn't reply because she was right.

Tina began to tell Carlos she was tired of her boyfriend which was a rich cat.

"How could you be tired of being with a rich cat," Carlos asked Tina?

Tina paused for seconds, moments of time within the days of their life.

"I want you to have his position, "Tina said.

"How could you be tired of a rich cat spending all their money on you, keep your boyfriend and all the things he has to offer, use him for what he's worth. If you play it cool with me everything will work out for the best. I treat all my girlfriends like queens," Carlos said. "Damn how many girlfriends you got," Tina asked. "I got about eight or nine," Carlos said as they both begin laughing.

"I like the way you carry yourself as a gentleman. You're the coolest dude I ever met. You should've been an actor on one of them old 70's pimp movie," Tina said, as they both begin laughing.

Although they both was ghetto that night they had meaningful conversation of intellect above and beyond the ghetto streets.

Over time Carlos start spending time with Tina son, talking him for walks in the park, and to other places.

Tina and Carlos would creep off and have sex from time to time. When they wasn't together they'd have late night phone conversations. Tina loved late night phone conversations.

"I wish you and I were in a relationship I'd suck your dick every night," Tina said.

Little Carlos dick got hard imagining Tina sucking his dick.

Carlos told Tina to meet him on the other side of town at this cheap Motel.

Once he arrived to the Motel to his surprise Tina was already parked in front of the Motel impatiently waiting on him.

As they went into the room Tina immediately undressed, he noticed that she had on the cutest see through lingerie set; she looked sexy in the lingerie.

"What made you wear this lingerie set, you ain't never wore no lingerie before, you need to start wearing lingerie sets every time we fuck," Carlos said.

"You should've told me you like lingerie sets, I'll wear lingerie for you all the time, I'll do anything for you," Tina said.

She reached into her pocket and pulled out a camera. She then told Carlos to take the entire film of her. Carlos didn't understand why she'd want him to take pictures of her in lingerie. It was because she was going to send them to her boyfriend in jail. He was only locked up for a violation of probation which he had to serve thirty days in the county jail.

Little Carlos began to get aroused watching Tina in her see through lingerie.

After he took twenty pictures and sat the camera down, she started sucking his dick. She used a lot of saliva as she sucked it she used her hand to jag him off her mouth was fantastic.

He'd talk to her sweetly, softly, complimenting her on how fantastic her mouth was.

When it was time to nut he nutted all over her face.

Within seconds moments of time his dick got right back hard as a brick. She took off her lingerie set and laid flat on her stomach.

"Tear this pussy up," Tina said.

All night he worked the pussy as he made orgasm come to life.

The morning as sun-light shined across their face she woke up to the smell of bacon and eggs and walked up and kissed him on the cheek.

Carlos wasn't a big kisser but he enjoyed it this time.

Carlos knew she was falling, falling in love.

As time progressed along Tina and Carlos begin spending lots of time together. Tina even took Carlos to places he never been before. She even took him to a massage parlor, and on a seven day cruise.

Tina enjoyed living life to the fullest, and even having Carlos by her side.

Carlos hadn't heard from Blondie in a while she was busy doing work in other states trying to downgrade crime. One day unexpectedly he got a call from Blondie. She wanted to see him.

Blondie came and picked him up wearing a skirt and a shirt filled with red roses she looked wonderful to him. She took him to her place as soon as he got in her place he lift up her skirt to his surprise she wasn't wearing any panties.

She started smiling and said come on let's do it.

Carlos paused and remembered that he had a x-pill in his pocket. He told Blondie hold on one moment as he went to the kitchen got some Champagne popped the pill, and chased it with the Champagne.

He fucked her against the wall one leg up, and one down.....

Afterwards to his surprise she had recovered five pounds of weed, which was great for him because he hadn't been working only because he couldn't find a

good connect. All his connects had bunk weed. He

opened one pound and could smell the aroma and

knew it would be potent.

Chapter 14

Bo-Diggla introduced Carlos to smoking Hydro, better

known as dro. Bo-Diggla was a major player that

socialized with different people. Dro wasn't easy to find

in the city, almost damn near didn't exist.

Bo-Diggla sparked up an already rolled blunt of dro, and didn't tell Carlos that it was dro. After a few pulls that's when Carlos realized it wasn't regular weed.

Once Carlos found out it was dro he fell in love as he'd inhale, exhale, as time prevailed.

Carlos was more than happy to be back working on his weed spot, but he wish he could've got a connect on dro. But Bo told him that it wont be easy to get pounds of dro, it was a hassle to even get a few bags.

Bo-Diggla, and Carlos smoked another dro blunt, afterwards went their separate ways.

As Carlos cruised in his car slowly through the hood smoking a small piece of dro blunt Bo gave him, he seen this female at the bus stop. He pulled up to the bus stop and noticed she was crying and he didn't bother to talk to her. He slowed the car down and looked and seen tears flowing freely down her face and pulled off. As he got a short ride away his inner conscious began speaking, like damn I wonder what's wrong with that girl, did she get into a fight with her boyfriend or something, he thought to himself. Maybe she need me for some consolation or simply for me to express encouraging words for her to whip the tears away to bring her happiness again. He made a U-turn and drove back to the bus stop in which she was still there her bus didn't come yet.

He rode up slowly and asked her if she was okay and did she need a lift. He assumed she'd say no because she didn't know him and he didn't know her. But she said, "yes can you take me to my aunties house out south."

As she got into the car she whipped her tears away. Carlos then asked her what's wrong with you, what are you crying for. "My momma and daddy got into a fight, and I tried to break it up and my dad slapped me," she said, as she started back crying.

Carlos reached into the glove department and grabbed a box of napkins and handed it to her.

"Girl whip them tears from your eyes, you're too cute to be crying," Carlos said.

He automatically put a smile on her face. Her name was Phyllis, she had a face and a body that was the illest.

"Could you stop at a liquor store so I can get me something to drink." Phyllis said.

"No problem, what do you drink," Carlos asked? "I drink Champagne and wine coolers, I've tried hard liquor before, I don't like it tho, I prefer more mellow drinks," Phyllis said. "Reach under your seat, it's a bottle of Champagne under there," Carlos said.

As she pulled the Champagne from under the seat she noticed that it was a bottle of Andre extra dry. Coincidently this was her favorite brand. Look in the glove department and grab two cups.

She began pouring him, and her cups of Andre, they continue to listen to Eightball, and MJG song Pimps at a low tone.

"Why did you get into the car with me without hesitating, I'm sure you was taught at an early age, not to trust strangers, "Carlos said. "Boy I've been knowing you ever since we begin living in the city," She said. "Where did you live before ya'll moved here," Carlos asked. "Me and my family moved from Phille," she said.

"I never seen you before how do you know me,' Carlos asked. "I see you almost every day either standing on your weed spot or riding with Bo-Diggla," she said.

Carlos began thinking to himself that in order for her to be checking me out for a year she must really like me.

Without Carlos having to ask she just told him she don't have a boyfriend.

"Most of my days are spent exercising or reading a romance novel or at work," she said. "So you like being romantic and shit," Carlos said as they both begin laughing.

"Where do you work at," Carlos asked? "I work at the county hospital helping people in the wheel chair, I'm a wheel chair attendant. I make sure people in the wheel chair are getting taking care of," she said.

"You look like you should be in college somewhere," Carlos said as she began smiling. "I have attended college in the past. I haven't been to school in a while cuz it's difficult to attend college, go to work, and maintain a daily life; some people do it, but I just can't. I do plan on going back to college in the beginning of next year," she said.

"What classes have you took," Carlos asked? "Boy watch out," she said. Carlos instantly hit the brakes hard almost hit a stray dog. "Boy you betta keep your eye on the road," she said. The stray dog ran off as the kept it moving.

"Yeah what was you saying," she said. "I was asking you what classes have you took at college," Carlos said. "Well I was majoring to be a Pediatrician, but the last classes I took were 3 English classes, English 101, English 102, and Public Speaking," She said. "Public Speaking that ain't no English course," Carlos said. "Yes it is," she said.

By the time Carlos and Phyllis was riding down the e-way. Carlos began to look at Phyllis closer in her face and noticed that her skin was blemish free. She looked so good to him in the future to come he'd nicknamed her beauty.

As Carlos pulled up to Phyllis aunt home Phyllis paused as she didn't wanna leave.

Before she got out the car he asked her could he come pick her up tonight. She said no but told him to come pick her up tomorrow once he got off work, she told him she wanted to go to the movies and she'll treat. Carlos laughed and gave her his cell phone number, and his mom home phone number, and told her to call him when she got off work.

As he drove from Phyllis auntie's house he visualized himself on top of Phyllis pounding away at her pussy.

After driving for a few minutes his cell phone rang; it was his mom, she needed help moving furniture.

Once he made it to his mother's apartment building this female he knew from grammar school named Rhonda was sitting in front of the building on a paint bucket. As he walked into the building he said hey to her and she said hey back and she automatically striked up a conversation. He was shocked that Rhonda actually did strike up a conversation, because he hadn't conversated with her since grammar school; whenever they'd see each other they'd just say hi and keep stepping.

She began reminiscing about grammar school days, and begin complimenting him on his appearance including his fresh outfit.

All while she was talking Carlos watched those juicy lips and cute face.

Rhonda was cute but a hoodrat.

"Remember I use to be your girlfriend in grammar school," Rhonda said. "Yes," he said. "I wish I was still your girlfriend," Rhonda said. "I do to," Carlos said. "Let's kick it later on if you can get away from your boyfriend," Carlos said. "I ain't got no boyfriend," Rhonda said.

Carlos agreed to kick it with her but really didn't want to kick it with her this night or any other night, he just agreed not to hurt her feelings. She wasn't on his level.

She told Carlos her number, he told her he'll come pick her up at 8pm that night, as they went their separate ways.

Once he made it to her house he immediately begin rearranging furniture.

As he moved the furniture to one place to another his mom would visualize him when he was a kid; she missed those days as when he was a kid. Since he had start running the streets she'd never see him at all.

After relaxing with his mother for hours he left her apartment to go get some weed to smoke, and to check on his weed spot, and the other joint.

As he approached his car it was as if he could sense someone following him. He looked back to his surprise it was Rhonda. Rhonda had been standing down stairs waiting on him for hours, she really liked him.

He knew she wanted to hang out and get fucked. He was getting ready to make up an excuse not to hang out with her. But he was like fuck it since she waited on me for hours, and if she that thirsty to get fucked let me give her what she's looking for.

As they entered his car she wanted to drop her panties right then, and there. He was like a superstar to her, and she was like his biggest groupie.

As they pulled off he'd hit bumps in street, and she didn't feel a thing she was impressed on how Carlos rode in luxury.

He placed on some slow music as they made their way to the liquor store.

He purchased a bottle of Champagne{Mumms} and some blunts.

He went to his own joint and get six bags, he wanted so many bags because he wanted to get high and tear the pussy up.

As they continued to ride she rolled the blunts up for him although she didn't smoke.

As she rolled the first one she even lit it up with the cigarette lighter in the car. As she lit the blunt she puffed on it twice simply to get it smoking.

"I thought you said you didn't smoke you doing a good job of it," he said. "No I don't smoke but I know how to smoke, I puffed on it just to get it smoking," she said.

She passed it to him and he begin smoking and drove the streets of downtown.

As clouds of smoke filled the inside of the car he begin to lay his p down, come to find out they had a lot in common.

"You know I been liking you since we were kids. When you was my boyfriend I wanted to do it to you so bad, but you never tried to do it," Rhonda said.

He knew right then and there she still wanna do it.

"Somedays I just use to stare out my window just to see you pass by. All my girls like you, they always be talking about you," Rhonda said. That made him feel real good.

These Ho's be sitting around stalking me and fantasizing of being with me, ain't that some shit, he thought to himself.

She didn't want to be just one of his Ho's, she wanted that main girl slot. But she knew he wasn't a one woman's man, and she knew he was out of her league. But in the back of her mind she was willing to do what it takes to be with him.

She wanted to impress him so she start telling him about her future goals. She had wanted to finish college, and get into real estate.

"A, let's get a room," Carlos said. "Naw let's go to my house, I told you I ain't got no boyfriend," she said. "Naw let's get a room, I'll pay for it," she said no she didn't want him to waste any money. Carlos wanted to get her in a room so he could fuck with no interruptions.

Once they pulled up to her apartment building he begin to look at Rhonda smiling knowing he was getting ready to tear the pussy up.

As they reached her apartment{304} as she opened the door they stepped in, Carlos noticed that the apartment wasn't very clean, nor did she have any furniture. As a matter of fact she only had one table in the living room that didn't have chairs. It was two men and one of her female cousins sitting on stacked crates at the table playing cards.

As he entered one of the two guys begin to ask him what he is and where he was from. "I ain't nothing, and I ain't from around here," Carlos said. Carlos wasn't really trying to kick it with them he looked at they clothes and seen they wasn't on shit dirty gangbanging ass niggas.

I should've got a room, Carlos thought to himself.

Rhonda and Carlos proceeded to his bedroom walking pass a bedroom in which the door was opened. He noticed that it was several women in there smoking the pipe. It was her momma and a few of her crack head friends. Rhonda was embarrassed as she quickly shut the door.....

When Rhonda and Carlos made it to her room he noticed that her room was neat. The floor was waxed, her bed was fixed flawlessly, military style, the inside of her closet was properly organized, as far as the clothing and shoes were concerned.

He laid on the bed and took off his shoes to relax. She locked her door and turned the radio on to a jazz station. The mood was perfected by Carlos being high, and by the melodies of the jazz. The jazz immediately started to boost Carlos high.

She cut off the room light and turned on her lamp. She then began to stare into Lil Carlos brown eyes, and it was as she could see the sunrise, making love as a thrill, a blast. Carlos began to tell her how much he really liked her.

He began to undress her in hopes of her not objecting, she didn't object or show any signs of resistance. After he took off all her clothes he noticed that her body was flawless, but her feet looked as they had been in a war. Carlos hated a bitch with ugly feet, or ugly hands. Her titties was perfect size, she had no stretch marks on her stomach or ass like the average Ho did.

He stood up staring at her body admiring the view for about 30 seconds. He knew that he was getting ready to fuck the shit out of her.

As he finished undressing himself he realized that due to the graphic nature of her apartment not being tidy that he should use a condom, in which he kept in his pocket. Lil Carlos was a dummy when it came down to having safe sex, but this evening he would participate in protective sex.

As he began to put the condom on she whispered in his ear, I like to get hit from the back.

He stood her up and got behind her and then she bent over and touched her toes as Carlos inserted his dick into the midst of her pussy. He gripped her ass cheeks as if he was trying to squeeze the life outta them and commence to long stroking, giving her all the dick.

As his dick in and out her pussy after many strokes she stood up unable to withstand the pain, but although she stood up he continued hitting that shit.

He began slapping her hard on her ass cheeks aggressively telling her to bend her ass back over. "I can't bend back over, your dick to big," she said. Then he begin slapping her ass cheeks harder, and hollering in a firm and fierce manner as he was a drill sergeant in the army....."Girl bend your hot ass over right now corporal Rhonda," he said. She felt right into play as if she'd been in the army before. "Yes sir, sergeant Carlos," she said as she bent right over.

As she bent over he begin hitting that shit harder. It felt so good it was as if the rubber had bust, but it didn't.

After minutes of long stroking her, he nutted. Normally it didn't take him a long time to nut, especially within a tight pussy. But it did take him a while to nut with Rhonda because he used a rubber.

He took his dick outta her pussy, she turned around with a devilish grin on her face and punched him in the chest slightly; "boy you didn't have to do it so hard," she said as he smiled and gave her no reply.

He fired up another blunt as the sounds of R.Kelly echoed from the speakers.

As Carlos proceeded to smoke he walked around the room still in the nude with his chest poked out like he had won a professional heavy weight boxers match, he felt great.

As Carlos was halfway through smoking the blunt, she laid on her bed, on her stomach with her ass in the air.....she looked back at Carlos genuinely smiling at Carlos and told him to come on.

She wanted to do it again.

He put the blunt out in the ashtray on top of the radio in the process of doing so he thought to himself, what is this ashtray doing on the radio and she don't even smoke.

As he began to approach her she then told him boy take it easy this time. He climbed on top of her placed his dick within her lovely pussy hole and begin fucking her hard and fast, but not as hard or fast as he did the first time. Each pump he'd adore the way her butt cheeks would bounce. To him, the sight of her ass cheeks bouncing up and down was phenomenal.

As he continued providing Rhonda with the dick she loved every minute of it.

He took a pause a smoke break, and Rhonda begin telling him again about what her plans was for the future and that she wanted to be with him.

They sexed for an hour on and off. Afterwards Carlos got his blunts and went to his weed spot to check on his money.

Once he approached his weed spot he came in contact with Tina, and Maryland, Tina was buying weed.

Tina offered Carlos to go clubbin with him, but he said no he had business to attend to. Tina talked him into it, he decided to go because he knew once it was over it would be hardcore sex going on.

They set a date to meet up in the hood in an hour.

Carlos went to his apartment to change clothes.

As he made it within his mother's apartment he entered the back room with no idea of what he was going to wear. He had enough clothes and shoes to open up a clothing store.

He decided to put on an outfit that matched his gator shoes. The outfit he decided to put on wasn't brand new. He wanted to put on an outfit that had creases in it, heavy starch from the cleaners.

He shitted, shower, shaved, and smoked one and put on his clothes ready to hit the town.

It took thirty minutes to get ready, but once he did he went right back to the hood.

Once he made it back to the hood he circled blocks looking for Tina, and Maryland.

Tina, and Maryland was no where to be found.

Carlos set in front of the liquor store waiting on Tina, and Maryland, he knew this was where they'd come looking for him at because this was a dope spot where all the guys hung out at.

Carlos sat in front of the liquor store for an hour waiting on the girls. He wondered if they'd went to the party without him. Tina didn't have a cell phone, and every time he called her house he got no answer.

He decided to go into the liquor store to get a case a beer, some snacks, and some blunts.

As he exited the liquor store he hung out with the guys for a little while. He didn't want to stand on a dope spot for a long time because he didn't feel like being hassled by the police, so he decided to sit back in the car.

As he sat in the car he blazed up another blunt thinking about all the money he'll be making from weed sells since Blondie would be back supplying.

Tina, and Maryland pulled up on the side of him, raised down their window, he raised down his, as Tina, and Maryland told him they was getting ready to park.

Tina, and Maryland wanted to ride with him because his car was luxury to them equipped with rims, and sounds.

The girls entered the car excited ready for party to begin.

Once they made it to the party Carlos noticed that the club was in a suburban area, and that all the cars were average; normally when he'd go to clubs the outside be like a car show.

Entering the city's police officers were there with hand held metal detectors to make sure anyone entering the club wasn't trying to conceal any dangerous weapons.

As the officer's move the metal detectors up, and down on the side of Carlos one of the officer's told Carlos, you're a lucky man three females just went in and the two girls you brought made five. Carlos heard him, but didn't pay attention to what he was saying.

Once Carlos actually made it all the way into the club he fell in love with the sight.....the inside of the club was filled with majority of women in their lingerie sets, or thongs and bra. Their were a few female in thongs with no bras on.

Tina, and Maryland already knew what type of party this was going to be, but they didn't tell Carlos, they left it as a surprise.

Tina, and Maryland immediately begin to strip as they entered the club. They stripped down to their panties, and bra. Tina pulled her panties in her ass to make them fit like thongs; she wanted to fit in with the other girls showing off their merchandise.

Carlos stood in the club paused as if he were stuck in time. He'd never been to a party like this. Nor did he ever see so many women all at the same time half naked. He looked around as if he was looking at a real live ghost or Aliens.

He looked at Tina, and Maryland with a small grin on his face. He began thinking to himself that he loved Tina, and Maryland for bringing him to this party.

He went to the bar to order four bottles of Rose, and a bottle of Patron. And he bought some Champagne glasses.

As he begin popping bottles with Tina, and Maryland he started to pass out Champagne glasses to any female that was nearby as he filled their glasses with

Rose.....He'd just came into the party and was already in the lime light.

He began to notice that it wasn't that many men in the party, which was strange to him. But he wasn't tripping, more Ho's he could try to come up with.

What Carlos didn't know was that the party was originally designed for and by Tina's ex high school male friends whom went on to college and earned a Master's degree in Math, and Computer Science. He was celebrating his success of finishing college by having this party.

He designed it that every five women get in then they'll let one man in; that way they would always have more women, than men.

It was a little bit over a hundred women, but only approximately 30 men at the party. None of the men were undressed.

Before long Carlos departed from Tina, and Maryland to socialize and bump Ho's.

Carlos stayed on the dance floor for a while dancing and partying like this was his last day on Earth, he was really enjoying himself.

After dancing for a while he went back to the bar and begin flashing money like it wasn't a thing..... buying drinks for strangers, tipping the bar tender and just having a good time. He began cracking jokes, hugging females and taking pictures by the photographer.

Carlos had forgot Tina, and Maryland even existed.

One thing Carlos liked about the party was that it was filled with females of different ethnic origins. Normally when he went clubbin it would be majority of black females. But this club was filled with blacks, whites, Latinos, and even a couple Chinese, that's because they had went to college with Roger.

After a couple hours Carlos was so drunk he could barely stand up.

Carlos left the bar staggering to the washroom. He was so drunk that he didn't pay attention to the sign on the door that it was the ladies room.

He went into the ladies room to piss, as he opened one of the stalls he came across two females having sex. It was a big fat black female with a strap on dildo fucking a white female from the back.

Carlos watched the action for a little while without them even knowing.

"Carlos was walking back to the bar and accidently bumped into this cute young lady. "Damn you just gone bump into me without saying excuse me," she said. "Forgive me, I apologize it was an honest mistake," Carlos said.

She began to talk to him, come to find out her name was Angie and she was currently in college for journalism. Although he was sloppy drunk Carlos still talked to her on her level Carlos was street but had a lot of game from Lisa about education, amongst other things.

She felt outta place at the party, but after minutes Carlos made her feel at home.

She was white but never had dated a black guy before, but she was interested in Carlos.

After approximately fifteen minutes of conversating Carlos, and Angie exchanged numbers and went their separate ways.....Angie left the party Carlos went back to the bar.

Carlos was already sloppy drunk but he still began to order repeated small shots of Gin. Usually when he drunk liquor he'd like to fire up blunts in the process, but by him being in this club he couldn't fire up any blunts. He ran across this one individual smoking small cigars the size of a cigarettes so he walked over to ask him what was he smoking, and asked for one of the small cigars which was good. Carlos then asked him where he got it from, he told him which stores sell them. Carlos put in a mental note that he would be going to that store on a later date.

After hours of partying Carlos leaned on the wall with Tina and Maryland admiring the view of all the half dressed ladies. To him this was better than a strip club.

As Carlos begin to walk he was so drunk he fell to his knees, and quickly got back up. Tina and Maryland lift him up put him on their shoulders and took him out the club.

Right when they got to the door Tina, and Maryland got dressed, and walked Carlos to the car.

Tina, and Maryland set fire to the blunt and smashed off.

Carlos awake to Tina and Maryland sucking his dick at the same time, he couldn't believe it. Tina paused looked up seen his was awake. "Good morning sleepy head," Tina said. Without responding Carlos pushed her head back down to the dick so she could continue

sucking.....

Chapter 15

As Carlos finished fucking Blondie, and getting a few pounds of weed from her, he got a call, to his surprise it was Lisa.

"I miss being with you, we don't never spend that much time together," Lisa said. Carlos was going to think of some good game, but decided to just go spend time with her. He dropped the pounds off at home and went straight to pick Lisa up.

They ended up going to see a play and back out to eat. Afterwards hardcore sex.

Proceeding that day he would go and see her on a more frequent level. He really liked Lisa she was cool.....

One day Carlos awoke out of a nightmare of being ate by Sharks and went to the bathroom to piss. Once he started pissing he could feel the pain of his dick burning like never before.....

Later the same day he told Bo-Diggla that his dick be burning every time he piss. Bo-Diggla told him he should go get tested because 9 times outta 10 he had gonorrhea.

He went to the free clinic come to find out he did have gonorrhea. He caught it from Tina after that he stop fucking with her. He called up and Blondie, amongst others told them to get tested come to find out they didn't have it.

After that scenario Carlos made sure to always use a condom.....

As Carlos and a couple of his homies sat at the table bagging up weed, he'd visualize all the money he was going to make, and all the money he will have if he stop

spending it flamboyantly.....

"I got a connect on the dro," Bo-Diggla said. "For real,"

Carlos said. "How much for a pound," Carlos asked? Bo

told him the price as his eyes got big. "I'm not paying

that much for no pound, that's crazy," Carlos said.

"That's how much it cost because you'll sell one blunt

for a sawbuck," Bo-Diggla said. "Be for real, who gone

pay ten dollars for a nickel bag," Carlos said. "Everybody

will because it's a bomb. Dro different from weed you'll

have to weigh each bag with the scale. Trust me bro you

going to corner the market don't nobody else got dro,

you'll be the only one with it," Bo-Diggla said.....

Carlos ended up buying a pound of dro to see what it

do. Him and Bo weighed each bag, and bagged it up,

passed out a few samples. In the days to follow his dro

spot was off the chain. He still kept his regular weed

spot, and continued to help Bo-Diggla with his spots. The next upcoming week Carlos had 20,000 stack, a couple weeks to follow he had 30,000 stack.

Carlos was glad he took Bo-Diggla's advice on buying dro.....

"Bo-Dig, I got 30 stacks," Carlos said. "30 stacks, stacked that's love. But you should never tell nobody how much money you got saved, and you should make people think you got less money than you do. If you got 30 stacks make people think you got 3 stacks. Never tell nobody how much money you got not even me, your own homies will be the ones to snake you or have their hand out," Bo-Diggla said, as Carlos paused in silence soaking up game for free.

Carlos got a call from his granny she told him she needed some help around her house whenever he got time Carlos decided to go see his granny right then and there she lived in the hood but he just didn't go over there that much.

Once Carlos made it to his granny's house he noticed that the door was unlock, he came in and seen his granny laying on the floor; while awake nightmares as if he was asleep flashed through his head of her death laying in a casket came to mind. He ran to her crying out granny. "Boy what is wrong with you," granny ask Carlos. "I thought something was wrong with you," Carlos. "No child thank the Lord that my body, mind, and soul is good. But when it's time to go I can't wait to meet the Lord on judgement day," Granny said.

Carlos felt so relief, words couldn't express the joy he felt inside.

Life is to short I gotta start spending more time with my granny, Carlos thought to himself.

After helping granny around the house Carlos spent the rest of the day with granny.

Granny would read to him church scriptures, and together they baked cakes, and cookies, and relaxed around the house.

Chapter 16

Carlos flipped another new car, a luxury car. He got it smoked out and went to pick up Lisa so she could tell him the best place to get auto insurance. He signed up for auto insurance over the phone it only took minutes, Carlos didn't know it was that easy.

After getting the insurance taking care of over the phone, Carlos, and Lisa decided to go to a poetry club it was both of their first time.

When they first stepped in the club it was small and real dark, almost everyone had on black. There were no standing because the club was filled with tables in which everybody was seated. A waiter showed Carlos,

and Lisa to a table.

Lisa ordered food, Carlos ordered liquor.

In no time flat the poets were hitting the stage, the

first poet was called Crisis, he performed a poem called

Stained Mirror: It was a stain in the mirror,

but yet and still she could see

things

clearer.

No Pilgrims or Happy

Thanksgiving,

but instead roaches that fell

from ceilings.

Gun shots of killings.

Abandon building living.

Mice that walked around as if

they rented.

Kris Kringle ponded gifts on

Christmas.

She'd bear witness to those that

got high

as the only way to achieve a

wonderful   prism.

Over packed prisons of those

that didn't

listen, didn't abide be the

fundamental

written guidance of the

literature.

She'd seen those before her

that made wrong

decisions, she'd let that be a

lesson

learned off others failed

missions.

Those that's telling the ones

secretly   planted kisses.

Obituaries of those we love

R.I.P. we miss   them.

Lives that was confiscated over

foolish and   petty issues.

She blanked out and broke all

mirrors,

more than seven years bad luck

superstition

would definitely continue.

Took a piece of the broken

mirror and slid   both of her wrist

tissue, couldn't live

the life of reality of a stain

mirror.

The next poet came, her name was Love she recited a

poem called white birds:

Lovely white birds fly from

palms

of hands, fly go far away.

Live to see another day.

In the skies with no limits

forever

stay.

Never perish away, even when

it becomes

the darkness after the light of

day.

Lovely birds don't let the other

birds

lead you astray,

fly, fly, far away go your

separate

ways.

Lovely white birds fly far away.

Stay in the sky forever at your

utmost

high.

Spread your wings high as the

sky.

Chirp lovely white birds, chirp

in the morning as the sunrise,

light up the skies, chirp and

forever fly,

to forever rise.

Lovely white birds fly.

Lisa, and Carlos would spend a lot of time together. Lisa would continue to preach to Carlos about getting his life on track and making the right decisions. To stop selling drugs and running the streets it was no future in it.

Carlos family, and older cats from the hood would also preach to Carlos about making the right decisions with his future to stop selling drugs and start doing the right things for his future.

Carlos didn't listen he kept being a bad boy as he'd see flashes of existence of family members and friends that were older than him graduating college, buying homes, and being happily married.

The days to come he began to explore life, traveling. Sometimes he'd travel with Lisa, sometime with other Ho's. He'd take vacation on cruises just him, and Lisa. After the cruises they'd travel to Vegas, Cancun, Florida, amongst other places when the money, and time was available.

By him being a teenager he was living life to the fullest, well at least that's what it seemed to him.

Bo-Diggla was proud of him, and kept telling him to continue stacking money preparing for a rainy day because you never know when a drought would hit, the feds come through grabbing people, or if you may need to bound out.

Chapter 17

As a few years progressed along Carlos was still performing in the streets getting money. More money than some of those twice his age. He found himself fucking more top flight Ho's. Ho's that had top flight careers, college educated, and top flight business owners, vets.

Carlos began to even start making more money than he was ever getting.

Until one summer everything came crashing down like a nightmare of a horror flick that came true.

One of the guys from the hood got killed, so the hood was waring heavy, like never before it was hard for Carlos workers to work and make money to much shooting, and the police was to hot because of the shootings. Homicide grabbed and locked up a few of his homies for murders, and a few of his homies got killed.

As a month and half followed the war was still going on but the shooting slowed down somewhat, the Feds came and grabbed part of Bo-Diggla's team, they had been selling kilos of cocaine to the Feds. Bo-Diggla was the only one the Feds didn't grab yet he was on the run from the Feds.

Carlos dro connect got killed, and it was hard to find another one. Bo-Diggla's joints was closed down since the Feds came through so Carlos wasn't getting any money, all the money he had stacked started to disappear as his cost of living was still expensive; by him steady spending money and not making money all his stacks stacked was started to come into non-existence.....

Carlos noticed how once the money had slowed down, how his friends and Ho's became into non-existence.

Carlos started smoking PCP, but they called it Leaf. The Leaf momentarily take away his pain of going broke; the Leaf made him feel like champions of mountains to climb. At times high off Leaf he felt above life as if he was walking on clouds.

One day he went to visit Bo-Diggla at Bo-Diggla's hide out. Carlos was the only one that knew where Bo-Diggla was hiding at.

Bo-Diggla never smoked Leaf but he'd been around he could tell that Carlos was high off Leaf. He snapped out on Carlos for smoking Leaf; Carlos explained to him what he was going through in life. Bo-Diggla told him it is what it is all the things you going through comes along with the territory. Carlos began to question Bo-Diggla about was he worried about the Feds. "Hell yeah, but it is what it is, it's no surprise to me this what comes with game. If the Feds ever find me and let me out I'll be in the streets clocking again," Bo-Diggla said.

Carlos remained silent thinking of the things Bo said, and the things he learned over the years.....

He left Bo, and went over to the hood. Carlos was so fucked up financially that he had to find a hustle. So he went to one of homies joint to run a shift. His homie let him run it; the day went by smooth the stick up man didn't come. The police sweated but didn't catch none of the workers.

As Carlos shift was almost at an end the police rode up two detectives jumped out their car searching Carlos, Carlos didn't panic one bit, because he didn't have any drugs or money on him. What Carlos didn't know was that the two detectives had been watching him for hours from a nearby abandon building.....

"Tell us where they holding all the work at, and I'll let you go," one detective said. "What work I'm just out here kicking it, ain't on shit," Carlos said. "Well we been watching you for hours, so if you don't tell us where the work is we locking you up," the detective said. "I don't know what you talking about," Carlos said.....

The detective grabbed Carlos handcuffed him and threw him in the back seat of the detective car and slammed the door.....

Carlos was high off Leaf in another zone, but still knew what was going on.

The police put a pack of blows on him.

Carlos went through processing at the police station, and was shipped to the county jail.

Once he made it to the jail on the unit, the guys screened him to see if he was plugged or not, as Carlos got with the program.

Carlos bond was 3,000 to walk. Carlos had only 500 hundred of his own money; he was trying to see who would come show love and bond him out.

Carlos sat in the county for a week, and knew he'd have to change his life prison was no place for him to be.

The guy Carlos was running the joint for put up a 1,000 and Carlos family put up the other 2,000; Carlos never told them he had 500 put up.....

Once Carlos was released he felt like he was coming home from doing 20 years in prison.....

Carlos started back hustling, but only regular weed. He didn't have a weed spot he'd just work off his phone;

when people wanted weed they'd call him give him a number of bags they wanted and he'd deliver; the money was slow not even close to what he was use to getting, but the little money helped him maintain.

He tried to get probation but that was out of the question, because he was already on probation for a pistol case.....

As months progressed along he ended up taking a plea for 4 years, off that 4 years he'd have to do 50% which left him to do 2 years. If he acted correctly and behaved himself in the joint he'd only have to do 18 months.....

Once he made it to the joint he was expected to see the inside as a hardcore prison like in the movies. To his surprise it was totally different. First of all there were no cells with bars it was cells with doors, and it wasn't hardcore it all, as a matter of fact the deck he was on was real peaceful; almost everybody either had a job or attending college.....

In no time he filled out to get his G.E.D. while completing his G.E.D. program he went on take college courses. Once in the school building he noticed that it was so cute flirty white chicks that worked in the school building.

A teacher's aide position became available that would give him the opportunity to earn some extra cash and to be around the Ho's; never in his wildest dream would he ever imagine he'd be embarking in sexual acts with female staff members.....

In the first months Carlos had Ho's writing him. After like the 4th month letters from Ho's became hardly ever. Now it was time for Carlos to see who his true friends was, and to see which chick really loved him. He seen for himself that none of them really loved him like he thought they did, because if they did they'd be right by his side in troublesome times.....

It's was this older white lady, the school secretary she was 50 years old but had a body like a Goddess, made the inmates fantasize. He personality was like a female version of Mr. Rogers, but she had game like a chick from the hood, maybe because she was older and had been working around inmates for a few years.....

She began to talk to Carlos on a more frequent level; she'd compliment him on his looks and his style. She start telling him how corny, and boring her husband was and that she needed some excitement in her life. Although she was older she had wanted to take a walk on the wild side like going to a nude beach for instance. She also she wanted a dope dealer boyfriend because she had heard how good dope dealers treat their girlfriends.

Carlos was smart he'd talk with her but would be selective on the words he chose he didn't wanna say or do the wrong thing to end up in seg. and sulfur from loss of good time.

As the weeks proceeded on she begin to open-up to Carlos more, and more of her personal feelings. She even told Carlos things she never told anyone else. By now it was obvious to Carlos that she liked him.

After a couple months Carlos, and the secretary was in the office alone and she asked him for a massage. Of course he gave it to her, and right then and there he knew someday he would be enjoying the warmness of her Vagina.

After a few more weeks past Carlos and school secretary was in the office alone, coincidently the other two office workers had called off that day. Carlos was there just simply to help her with some paper work.

What Carlos didn't know was that her pussy was yearning to be pounded away because her husband had a little dick, and she was yearning to get her pussy beat up. She'd never been with a black guy before but she'd always fantasize, because she had heard the false myth about black guys having big dicks.

Carlos was in another part of the office when the school secretary Mrs. Starks came in to use the copy machine. Like in the movies she stumbled off a cord almost fell to the ground as Carlos caught her. He caught her in a way that she felt frontwards in his arms. She landed in his arms as she rested there as they looked into each other eyes with a slight grin on their faces. She kissed him. Carlos couldn't believe it. After a short kiss she snatched her lips away from him in disbelief, she couldn't believe she just kissed him.

She attempted to get released from Carlos arms by slightly pushing him away..... Carlos grabbed her tightly around the waist and forcefully, yet passionately kissed her, she enjoyed every second of it. Without second guessing it he bent her over on the desk and pulled up her skirt and snatched her panties off and commenced to fucking her from the back as he adored the way her white ass jiggled.

This was the best fuck Mrs. Stark ever had; while Carlos continued hitting the pussy

from the back she attempted to stop the action because the pain of his dick was hurting her. But Carlos had a lock on her in which she couldn't get released.

In no time Carlos was nutting in the pussy.

"Leave, please leave," Mrs. Starks said, as Carlos ran fleeing the scene.

Carlos swiftly made his way back to the unit confused, and scared. I thought she was getting ready to scream rape.....

The next morning as he awoke he was pleased; because he knew if he was in any trouble they would've got him yesterday, as a matter of fact they would've got him right then and there after the incident occurred.

As he went to his teacher's assistant assignment and was puzzled on how to approach Mrs. Starks. Soon as she walked in the classroom she began to smile as her smile would light up the world. She immediately walked up to him shook his hand and told him good morning. He then knew that it was getting ready to be the beginning to be beautiful friendship.

Later on that day as Mrs. Starks and Carlos was alone she told him to never tell anybody she didn't want to lose her job. Of course Carlos wasn't going to tell anybody.

All the rest of the day when they had the chance to be alone, they would just gaze into each other eyes.

She loved having rough sex with Carlos, she wish her husband had a big dick and could fuck like Carlos.

In time every time they was alone they'd kiss as a daily shine, or talking making love to each other's mind. They did have sex from time to time, but they couldn't do it very often because they might get caught. But when they did have sex it was rough, hardcore and nasty.

Over time Carlos convinced Mrs. starks to start sucking his dick, and she was so good at it.

Eventually Mrs. Starks fell in love with Carlos she even considered divorcing her husband to be with Carlos once he was free. But she figured that would be a bad idea, because she was married to her husband for years whom was the father of her two kids. And she knew Carlos would probably return back to the streets.

More and more Mrs. Starks begin to talk to Carlos about sexual desires. For Carlos although he was stuck in prison being around her freed his mind.

Mrs. Starks told Carlos she'd wanted to get gang bang by many men but she'd never do it because she was married. Hearing that was strange for Carlos because most women wanted a threesome not a gang bang. He asked her if she would do a threesome with another woman, she said she'd never have sex with another woman under no circumstances.

She loved sucking Carlos dick, her husband wouldn't allow her to suck his dick or eat her pussy, well at least not often he claimed he didn't want to have his wife perform oral sex on him and have to kiss her in the mouth later on down the line.

Mrs. Starks loved when Carlos stood her straight up and fucked her squeezing her titties as firm as he possibly could. Normally when they did get a chance to fuck she did suck his dick afterwards without him having to ask.

Being around Mrs. Starks Carlos understood why black guys would marry white chicks. Mrs. Starks was caring, sweet, loving, genuinely nice, more than any other chick he ever fucked with.

After Carlos having the job for 7 months the prison school system was shut down due to lack of finance within the state's budget; therefore Mrs. Starks had to leave to find another job outside of the prison.

Carlos tried to convince her to get up with him once he got out, she said no it was over she was married, but she wished him the best of luck in life in general.

A few months later the state started back funding the prison school system. A few of the other staff members came back, Mrs. Starks never came back she found her a higher paying job outside of the prison.

Carlos, and Mrs. Starks really missed one another. Throughout time they'd never forget or never regret their secret love affair.

Carlos never told anyone about him, and Mrs. Starks, besides who would believe him.

Chapter 18

As time progressed along there was still no letters from Ho's

One day out of the blue unexpectedly Carlos got a letter from one of his old Ho's from the hood, all said news: Three of his homies were killed. Two of his other homies, had did a murder and got caught with the smoking guns, therefore they'll never see the streets again. And that the Feds finally caught Bo-Diggla. Behind close doors he shed a blood stain of tears that would forever haunt him throughout his livelihood of years.

Carlos immediately left his cell got on the phone and called to confirm if the Feds had caught Bo-Diggla or not, and it was true they did.

Carlos knew of many scenarios where the Feds had got people and they never seen the streets again, Carlos hoped that this wouldn't be one of those scenarios.

As Carlos continued to talk to his homie over the phone, his homie told him of others that had got killed that the female didn't put in the letter, and that this chick they grew up with was dying of A.I.D.S. Wow, Carlos thought to himself.

Carlos inner soul cried out.

Carlos went right back to his cell stared at the walls in silence, and decided to write Bo-Diggla a letter. He couldn't write Bo-Diggla straight forward the joints didn't allow inmate to inmate letters, so he wrote a letter and sent it to his mom to send to Bo-Diggla.

Once Bo-Diggla received the letter he seen the name on it, and didn't know who it was from. He opened it, read it, and came to find out, it was Carlos. In his cell he began to jump for joy.

He immediately wrote Carlos back expressing his gratitude to Carlos for taking time out to write him a letter, and that Carlos should make the right decisions in life upon his release so he wouldn't end up like him. Bo-Diggla went on to tell Carlos the Feds offered him eight years, but he didn't take it he was trying to get lesser.

Once Carlos received his letter he felt a great sign of relief, knowing Bo-Diggla wasn't going to be trapped in the system of the prison prism.....

Chapter 19

One day Carlos got a letter from an unknown name. He assumed that it was a letter from Bo-Diggla in which he sent to one of his girlfriends to send to him. Once he opened the envelope and pulled out the letter and began to read it he became aware that it was one of his old Ho's. It was Tasha whom he had fucked years ago, and she wanted him as a boyfriend but he didn't take her serious.

Tasha had got his address from his cousin. She really liked Carlos, and wanted them to be together as one.

In no time Carlos and Tasha was exchanging letters on a frequent level, and she started visiting and sending money. Carlos started to fall in love, not just with her, but in love with the way she treated him.

Tasha had did a lot of growing up over the years, she had two kids by a deadbeat dad. She had a high paying job, nice apartment, and owned a car; Carlos was impressed.

If Tasha stayed around being supportive until he got out, she would definitely be the one Carlos would be with upon his release.

One day Carlos got a letter from Bo-Diggla, Lisa, and Tasha. He read Lisa's letter first because he hadn't heard from her in a while. Lisa wrote him simply because she had him on her mind, and decided to drop him a few lines. The letter was asking him how he was doing, and to keep his head up, and stay focus on the right track to do positive things with his life once he got free from prison. Carlos wrote her right back; a short letter that was all heartfelt.

Next he read Bo-Diggla's letter; Bo-Diggla was mentioning that he was in there maintaining and couldn't wait until he had a projected out date so he could know exactly when he'd be free.

Tasha letter was heart warming, love; she'd express to Carlos on how much she loved him, and couldn't wait to he was free so they could be a family together, her, him, and her sons. She ended up mentioning to Carlos in the letter that she'd start fingering herself as she had constant visions of him beating the pussy up, and that she'd fantasize about being raped in the ass. And that ever since she could remember she enjoyed just watching others fuck. Her letter turned Carlos on drove him wild inside. He couldn't wait to the next time they talked to have phone sex.

Periods reoccurring conditions and events carried on for Tasha, the deeper love felt, as father times clocks ticks away as time melt, the greatest love, and joy became a blessing to be dealt.

Throughout the rest of his stay in prison Tasha continued to remain with him a loyalist.

As Carlos quit his assignment as a T.A. starting attending college courses, and having the pleasure to rotate with Tasha time flew by. In in days of life no matter what people got going on time waits for no men.

Chapter 20

Before Carlos knew it his prison sentence was almost over he had only a couple weeks left to go before go before going home, as the sounds of bells would ring in his head, as he'd constantly hear the voice of Dr. Martin Luther King Jr. saying let freedom ring, repeatedly.

Carlos mom amongst others would talk to Carlos about doing the right things upon his release. Carlos assured everybody that he wouldn't be returning to the streets or being involved with any criminal activities.

Carlos mom asked if he wanted a coming home party he said no because he didn't want to be around the fakes, the phonies whom showed no love.

On his release date Tasha came to pick him up, as their tongues collided in which seemed as an everlasting eternal kiss; they kissed as if they were actually French.

Carlos mom wanted him to parole to her house but he decided to parole to Tasha's place he wanted to lay up and enjoy the pleasure of hardcore erotica to it's fullest extent.....

As they drove down the highway both of them quiet listening to rhythm, and blues gazing at the sun visualizing the product of love that became, mutual loving one in the same.....

After driving for about thirty minutes Tasha drove by a Motel, and decided to stop there, she was more anxious than Carlos to have nasty sex, being that she hadn't had it such a long time.

Once in the Motel room they didn't say a word they both undressed in 0.3 seconds as she laid on her back he climbed on top of her. "Put my dick in your pussy," he told her in low tone, as she obeyed his order. As he slammed his dick in out her pussy it was as if he was mad at the world, he tore the pussy up.....

"Give me this pussy, give me this pussy, give me this pussy," he said in each and every hard stroke as his dick stomped the pussy as she moaned usssss owwww ussss owwwww.

She loved being mistreated during sex which he didn't know and he'd come to find later on she liked being called bitches and choked. If she wasn't getting mistreated in the bedroom it was boring to her.

Once it was time for him to nut he unleashed it on her stomach and started tongue kissing the pussy as if it was an actual mouth as she begged him not to stop. "Please don't stop it feel so good," she said repeatedly.

He turned around and put his dick in her mouth as she ate his dick he ate her pussy at the same time, Carlos enjoyed doing it like that.....

She ate his dick thoroughly, she was sucking it so good that she'd move her head to the side each time the dick went in and out her mouth as if she was trying to suck the skin off his dick. Before long he begin fucking her mouth as if it was an actual pussy and choking her mouth with his dick she loved it.....

They sexed for about an hour on and off, majority on instead of off. Afterwards they got into the shower and washed each others body, and they continued on their journey home.

After hours of driving once they made it back to the city they ended up at his mom's apartment as they knocked on the door as his mom opened it she was happy to see him, his mom had the same feeling as t the day he was born. Once Carlos made it inside the house he noticed the table filled with lots of home cook food, and ten other family members was there.

"I know you didn't want to have a party but this is your family," Joanne told Carlos.

"No problem mom I'm grateful that they're here," Carlos said.

As they said a prayer and sat down to eat Carlos begin to tell everybody about his expectations on his future. He had got a certificate in Electronics and was planning to work in that field coincidently his auntie Christine knew of an electronic company that was hiring, and didn't do background checks.

For hours Carlos chilled out with the family until it was time for him, and Tasha to go home.....

Once they made it home Carlos and her immediately undressed, and starting fucking.

As he hit the pussy from the back this time it was as if the both of them were in paradise. "Give me this pussy," Carlos said repeatedly as he tore the pussy up.

The next morning Tasha woke up before Carlos and went into the bathroom to attend to her hygiene.....

Afterwards she went into the kitchen to fix Bacon, and Eggs.

Carlos woke up to the smell of Bacon, and Eggs; to him the smell was wonderful.

Once Carlos reached the kitchen he seen her standing there in the nude, cooking. She knew that once he seen her in the nude he'd be ready to fuck.

Shortly once the Bacon, and Eggs were ready he bent her right over and fucked the shit outta her from the back.

He nutted in her and told her he loved her and ate his Bacon, and Eggs sandwich.

Later that day Carlos parole officer came to see him. To his surprise it was a female, a tall black thick cougar; Carlos was still a player and he wondered if he would have a chance at getting the pussy.

His parole agent read to him his stipulations on being on parole. He must not use drugs, not get caught by the police, and not move into another residence without informing her first. Carlos signed the documents in agreement as she left she grinned as if she was interested in him, and told him, "I'll see you next month."

Living with Tasha he thought that it would be a problem because of her two sons; on the contrary it was the opposite her sons loved him, which made Tasha love him even more.

After several weeks Carlos was hired in the electronics company that his auntie gave him the information to. His task would consist of him traveling to large stores to fix Electronics, and do wiring work in light fixtures.

The job paid lots of money. Carlos earned fat checks.

This was the first time Carlos worked a regular job. To Carlos it was wonderful he was able to get fat checks didn't have to worry about the police or other things that came along with running the streets.

Also this was Carlos first time being faithful to just one woman, although he seen other chicks that he'd love to smash he still remained faithful for the time being.....

Chapter 21

Carlos began hanging back with his old homies. He

didn't hang in the old hood, because he knew the chaos

and madness that goes on in the hood. When he'd hang

out with the guys from the hood it'll be outside of the

hood, like clubbin, ball games and other things of that nature. While hanging with the guys or just in general he never cheated on Tasha once, and made sure that he went home every night even if it was late.

One night at an exclusive club downtown Carlos noticed lots of flyers in the club that he'd been seeing in other areas outside the club around town. The reason he recognized the flyers is because they possessed an old school 70's player on it with a big ass old school hat on. He was at the club drunk as hell and decided to read it. He read it and came to find that in a few weeks there would be a players ball. The players ball would consist of all players to competition to see whom was the coldest player. Famous players would be there such as Don-Juan, Ice-T, amongst others. The players ball was design for any men that considered themselves a player.

The prize would be awarded to the player of the year which would be 1,500. Carlos was interested in the money but more interested in simply being recognized as being the player of the year.....All night he fantasized of being awarded, rewarded the player of the year. This would be like a dream come true for him. But he knew he didn't stand a chance of winning up against Don Juan, and Ice-T. Contrary to popular beliefs of not standing a chance on winning the contest against famous players, he still felt that he was one of the coldest players that ever exist. Although impending his release from prison he hadn't been on no player shit, he was faithful to Tasha.

As strange as it seems the day before the player's ball all that was interested in being in the contest would have to take a survey. The survey would be judged by a female panel, per-se; they females would pick who was fit for the contest, and who wasn't. Also the females would judge the contest to see who was the coldest player.....

The survey would consist of such questions of how do you treat women, and what do you like most about women amongst other things that revolved around women.

Once each player took a handwritten survey, the survey would have a number instead of a name; they did it that way because they knew if they put the names on it the females would probably pick the most popular player because of the name.

The next day the host of the club called Carlos over the phone, and told him he would be a contestant in the player's ball.

Carlos immediately put together an old 70's player's outfit.

The contest would be held a week later at the same club of course.

Carlos anxiously awaited for the week to come as a kid waiting on Christmas.

As the next week came about Carlos entered the club and noticed that the line was longer than any line he'd ever seen in life awaiting to get in. He also noticed while waiting in line there was Blacks, Latinos, Whites, and even a few Orientals which was strange to him because this particular club was normally occupied by many black; this particular day different races came together to see the players unit to compete.

As Carlos stepped in the club high off dro, and high feeling as if he was walking upon the clouds, he stepped in the club the entire scenery was phenomenal. Most, if not all of the men and women there dressed up in 60's, and 70's clothing. Players came from far, and wide to feel the love, the vibe.

By Carlos being a participant in the players ball he didn't have to wait in no lines, security let him right in.

Once Carlos made it within the club security escorted him back stage because he had a backstage pass due to him being in the players ball.

Once he made it backstage the first individual he seen was Don-Juan. He walked over to Don-Juan shook his hand, and then hugged him. He then greeted all the rest of the players including Ice-T. This was one of the best days of his life. Before the players actually took to the stage to compete they took pictures together, then they traded some of their past player stories, prayed and then prepared to hit the stage.

It was 12 females that would rate whom was the coldest player of the year. Outta the 12 women, 6 was Black, 3 was White, 3 was Latinos.

It was the time for the players to take the stage. Their first test was to come out one by one to model their outer wear. The D.J turned on the music, a song by Jay-Z titled Who You With as each player hit the stage modeling their outfits. All the players wore old 70's outfit.

The next task: The judges would say a different word to each player and he must think of a slick rhyme, quick, fast, and in a hurry. When it came to Carlos the judges said tree. "Just like a tree it always room to grow, women are full of beauty, beautiful, for ladies are heroes," Carlos said.

The next task was for the players to express how they felt about a woman that was overweight or unattractive.

The next task was for the players to express how they felt about domestic violence, which was odd because a lot ex-pimps use to beat up on their Ho's as a natural routine.

Proceeding those task they had to answer more questions on a paper with numbers on it instead of names so the judges wouldn't play favoritism to certain players.

They last task was for the player to model their outfit on the stage this time one by one and then step to the mic and speak of any player shit they desired.

At the end of it all Carlos won the player of the year award, he couldn't believe it that he won over Don-

Juan, and Ice-T. Don-Juan came in second place, a younger player in his early twenties came in third. Ice-T couldn't believe that he didn't win or even came in second or third place. But he had no jealousy or envy in his heart, nor did Don-Juan they all walked up to Carlos shaking his hand congratulating him.

"You one coldest players I ever met," Don-Juan whispered in Carlos ear.....

Chapter 22

7 months out of prison, and Carlos remained on the right track; only thing is that he'd continue to get high knowing if his parole agent ever dropped him he'll be in some trouble, luckily after the first couple months she stopped dropping him. Carlos continued to get high but only off weed, and pills while in prison he promised hisself he'd never smoke Leaf ever again in life.

Since his freedom he always made sure to keep in contact with Bo-Diggla, money orders, letters, pictures, and phone calls. Bo-Diggla had several years left Carlos couldn't wait to Bo got out to unite with his best friend.

One day Carlos was coming home from work and got in a gridlock, and decided to take a different route. Ironically he got caught in traffic and was stuck by a motel. Parked in the motel parking lot was a car the same as Tasha, he then noticed a kid's sticker in the back window the same as Tasha. He figured that couldn't be Tasha car, because once they made Tasha car they made many others, same model.....

The next day coincidently he took the same route to avoid the heavy traffic, once again a car that look like Tasha was there. He got out and looked at the license plate, and looked inside the car, and yes it was Tasha's car.

He parked in the cut awaiting for Tasha to come out she came out holding hands with her baby daddy Carlos heart was broken. He pulled off without them seeing him rushing home. On his way home he remembered the golden rule his dad, and Bo-Diggla taught him, never, ever trust a Ho.....

He went home confused not knowing how to deal with the situation.

All along I planned on marrying her and she been out getting fucked by her baby daddy, who knows how many times, he thought to himself.

Once she made it home she tried to kiss him, and she wanted to fuck but he shut her down, she didn't understand why because Carlos always wanted to fuck, he loved to fuck.

Carlos left went to the liquor store got a pint of Vodka slowly cup after cup drunk the entire bottle with no chaser.....

Later on that night he decided to fuck her but he beat the pussy up and fucked her in the ass with no Vaseline.

He didn't eat the pussy that night afraid he'd beating

her baby daddies nut out of it.....

Carlos decided to never tell her nor anyone else that

he caught her cheating. But from that day forth he

began to treat her like shit, and cheat on her constantly.

After several months went along him, they broke up

she was tired of him treating her like shit.....

Carlos moved out her apartment, and found him his

own apartment on the other side of town. Carlos made

a vow to himself to never fuck back with Tasha again,

not even for the sex she ruined that, but he'd forever

appreciate the love she showed him while he was in

prison.....

Chapter 23

Carlos decided to attend college he wanted to further his education so he could be equip with tools he needed to survive in this world of Macro, and Micro Economics.

His first class in college was an English course called Public Speaking; it taught students how to prepare and recite speeches. Informative speeches, Persuasive speeches, amongst other form of speeches which basically taught the students how to speak properly in front of an audience.

He became intrigued with this older lady named Haley.

One day Haley was in front of the class expressing a persuasive speech. The speech consist of persuading women to be more considerate of their male companion.

Carlos really enjoyed her speech. After class that day he walked up to Haley, and introduced himself. As they begin to conversate he noticed that Haley had the prettiest light blue eyes, and long Blonde hair. Haley reminded him of the old lady he use to fuck when he was in the joint.

As Haley talked he noticed that she had a unique way to express herself. Her nature seemed genuine, and naturally nice.

As Carlos and Haley begin to become friends only within school and not outside of school Haley and Carlos begin to open up more to one another. Carlos came to find that she had been divorce for five years, and hadn't dated since her divorce. The first thing came to Carlos mind is that she ain't fucked in five years. She had one child a daughter in Harvard studying law. Haley had already had her degree in hydroculture, and she was the owner of two flower shops, she told Carlos if he ever needed a job she could provide one for him. Haley was taking college classes to past time and simply to get an higher learning about life.

As time progressed along they begin to get better acquainted within school, to a point she'd actually hug him before and after class. Little did Carlos know she'd been liking him before he introduced himself to her in the past, and once school was over she'd think of him all day every day. She wanted Carlos to be her lover instead of her friend.

Haley had a twin sister named Katie. Carlos met Katie the same semester in math class. The first time he met Katie he assumed he was talking to Haley. The second time he seen Katie he wondered why she wasn't so friendly as she'd normally be, and he noticed that she changed clothe within the same day; he questioned her about her clothes being changed and that's when he found out it was her twin sister, and that's why Katie didn't talk to him a lot. But once Carlos told Katie he was close friends with her sister that's when they hit it off well.

"I want to tell you a secret, but you must promise not to tell a soul," Katie said. "I Promise," Carlos said. "My sister is tired of just be friends with you at school, she wants a relationship with you, she really likes you," Katie said.

The next day in Public Speaking Carlos walked up to Haley and asked her why she didn't tell him she had a twin sister. "I don't know it never cross my mind," Haley said.

After class Carlos invited Haley to this small cafe which was thirty minutes away from the school, she trailed him in her car.

Once they sat down at the table awaiting the waiter Haley would look into Carlos eyes it was as if she could see the sunrise.

Haley was over joyed to be going out with Carlos she knew it would soon lead into a beautiful relationship.

Although Haley was white and twice Carlos age he still really liked her, and vice versa.

After they ate at the Cafe they exchanged numbers and went their separate ways.

Later that night Haley couldn't cease to think of Carlos.

She hesitated to call him over the phone, because she didn't want to seem to eager.

After a while of debating to herself. She dialed the number and let the phone ring four times confused as she was on the verge of hanging up until Carlos answered. "Hello," Carlos said. "Can I speak to Carlos," Haley said. "This is Haley I just called to make sure you made it home safe," Haley said. "Yes Haley I made it home safe, but anyway did you start your homework," Carlos asked. "No, not yet, maybe I'll start and complete it tomorrow.

"You know anytime you need some help let me know," Haley said. "Likewise," Carlos said. "I'm glad that I have you in my life," Haley said. "It's a coincidence that you called me I was just getting ready to call you. For some strange reason I just can't stop thinking about you, you just look so good to me. Outta all my lifetime I've never met such a profound woman such as yourself. You're someone I can see myself marrying in the future," Carlos said.

Although Carlos was running game, Carlos words made Haley feel as the best woman that ever existed.....

As they continued to talk over the phone more and more she'd tell Carlos about herself. She told Carlos that ever since she laid eyes on him she knew he'd be the one for her, and she really meant that.

As they continued to talk over the phone Carlos assumed she wanted to get fucked that night, but she wasn't on that.

Carlos asked her if she needed him to come over and keep her company she said no not tonight, but in a polite manner.

From that day forth Carlos, and Haley would spend time together after class, and talk on the phone each day.

They'd attend events together going places like the Opera, horseback riding, health clubs to exercise, and poetry clubs, and doing other things of that nature. By her being an older white chick she wasn't interested in concerts or clubbin.....

After the 3 weeks of them being together Carlos just knew it would be hard to get the pussy, each time he'd try she'd shut him down.

He always passionately kissed her, her kisses were sweet like cherry. One night after they came back from the Opera as he walked her to her door she kissed him; as the their tongues coincided in the game of French kissing love under the full moon up above, she placed his hand on her ass. Although she was a white chick she had a big ass similar to the young black chicks in music videos. She stop kissing him for a brief moment in time, and told him softly to squeeze her ass. With both of his hands Carlos squeezed both of her ass cheeks and started back tongue kissing and sucking on her lips as the sweetness of her mouth became like a little kid craving for candy.

She fumbled with her keys frantically trying to get the door open. Once she got the door open she held his hand led him up the stairs to her bedroom.

Once inside her bedroom she left the light off but opened the curtains slightly so she could make love under the Moon.

Carlos kissed her, and then paused as he undressed her slowly admiring her wonderful nude body, her ass was so fat round and nice, flawless in his eyes. Her titties were so big nice and round. He undressed her laid her on the bed, held her legs in the air, and begin tongue kissing, eating the pussy to the best of his ability he wanted to get her sprung. Afterwards as he held her legs in the air he inserted his dick gently in and out the pussy. Once the pussy was wet he noticed that it was tight like a virgin. He always thought Tasha had the best pussy, Haley pussy was better. He slammed his dick in and out the tight wet pussy, and she'd moan and repeatedly say oh my gosh it feels so good. In no time he was busting nuts in her gut. He told her to lay flat on her stomach, as it took seconds for his dick to get back hard he had to force his dick back in the tight pussy as he slammed his dick in and out the pussy he adored the way the white ass cheeks would jiggle.....

About a week later for the first time she sucked his dick her mouth was so wet, moist and fantastic, above average.

One day Haley was alone watching this movie titled Unfaithful starring Diane Lane. She gave Carlos a call and asked him to come over never in his wildest dream would he ever imagine that he was getting ready to have aggressive sex.

Once Carlos made it over there she told him that she had been watching the movie Unfaithful, and she wanted to try some of the things that were in the movie. First thing she wanted to do was be aggressive and slap and beat on his chest during sex.

They got undressed as he laid on top of her she asked him if she could slap him. He said yes, not knowing that she would slap him hard as hell; she slapped him so hard he almost slapped her back, but he caught himself. Instead he forced his dick in her and took his anger it out on her pussy, that's what she wanted. As he beat the pussy up she'd moan loudly beating his chest saying your dick is to big your hurting me you animal you.

From that day forth he knew she was like other girls he dated she wanted hardcore rough sex.....

Once the semester was over Haley, and Carlos completed their college classes and didn't sign back up for anymore college classes next semester, because they was more interested in spending more time together.

Carlos even moved in with Haley, but he never gave up his apartment.

When he wasn't at work, and when she wasn't at the flower shop they'd always be together.

Both of them were in love. They'd never knew a love like this before.....

Chapter 24

Haley began to tell Katie of her and Carlos personal
sex life. By Haley and Katie being twin sisters they
always shared their personal life with each other. But
they'd never shared secrets of their sex life until Carlos
came along.

Katie use to act like she wasn't interested in hearing about their sex life when along she was over excited. Haley would tell Katie that all the time they were in doors they'd walk around in the nude. And that Carlos could have her body in anywayh and anytime he wanted it.

Haley would tell Katie how Carlos would have rough sex with her in the back of Katie's mind she wanted rough sex as well.

One day Katie told Haley that she was bored living home alone and that she wanted to move in with her, and Carlos.

Later that day Haley broke the news to Carlos, she thought Carlos would object, but it was no problem at all.

The following week, Carlos and a few of his homies helped moved Katie in.

After months of living together Katie would always find a way to get physical with Carlos. Normally she'd just hug him for long periods of time we they were alone. Eventually she started sitting on his lap. Right then and there Carlos knew that Katie wanted some action.

Eventually everywhere Haley, and Carlos went they would take Katie with them.

More and more Haley would tell Katie of their sex life. How Carlos would talk dirty to her during sex which sparked up their sex life. And that Carlos had a big cock.....

One day Carlos and Katie was home alone, and Katie called Carlos once he made it upstairs he noticed that

Katie wasn't in her room. Katie called Carlos again her voice came from the bathroom. Carlos walked to the bathroom push the door open and Katie was standing in there asshole naked looking in the mirror shaving under her arms. He paused in shock but pleased with seeing her naked.....

"Katie why would you call me in the bathroom while you were naked," Carlos asked? "Come in I need you to shave my back," Katie said. "I will once you put your clothes on," Carlos said. "Come in your like family to me, besides it's not like you haven't seen a naked body before," Katie said. "Once you put your clothes on I'll definitely will come shave your back," Carlos said.

Katie slipped on her panties, and bra. Once she put her panties and bra on Carlos came in to shave her back. As he shaved her back, he talked to her about her action, letting her know he was in love with her sister and wanted to marry her someday. Therefore she'd have to stop her action sitting on his lap, and calling him to the bathroom while she was naked.....

"I do all these things because I'm comfortable around you," Katie said. "No Katie you want some action," Carlos said as she began laughing.

"Now if I wasn't with your sister I'd definitely be interested in you," Carlos said.

"That's why I moved in with you and Haley because I want you," she said, as Carlos dropped the razor not knowing what to say or do.

"But Katie we can't," Carlos said. "I see the way you look at me, you want me to," Katie said.

"But I love her and wouldn't want to cheat on her, and I wouldn't want her to cheat on me," Carlos said. "How do you know she's not cheating on you at this very moment women are more slicker when it comes to

cheating, besides what goes on between you, and I

stays between you, and I," Katie said.....

Katie took her bra, and panties off before long Carlos

found himself naked on top Katie pounding away at her

pussy.....

Chapter 25

Approximately six months went by and Carlos, and

Katie were still secret lovers, and both had fell in love

with one another. But Carlos knew he would have to

put it to an end, because although he was in love with Katie, and loved Haley more, and wanted Haley to be his future, and his wife in the future.....

"Katie we got to put love affair to an end," Carlos said. Katie began snapping out slightly beating Carlos in the chest telling him that if he ever decided to put their love affair to an end she'd definitely tell Haley everything. Right there in the living room Carlos bent her over on the couch pulled her pants down, and panties off and with his left hand held her down, and started slapping her ass cheeks hard and firm as she pleaded for him to stop; proceeding he slipped his pants and boxers down and gently placed his dick in her pussy and fucked the shit out of her.

They ended up in the bedroom sexing as the tension between them had calmed down.

Outta nowhere Carlos heard a car pull up in the driveway. He looked out the window and it was Haley. Damn she home early Carlos thought to himself. Him, and Katie panicked as he slipped on his boxers and t-shirt and ran to him, and Haley's bedroom.

Haley walked up the stairs saying honey I home. As she entered their bedroom there Carlos laid on the bed as if he had been yearning for the tenderness of her touch forever and a day, genuinely without dismay seemed as if love shined his way.

"I'm glad you are home, I've been missing you," Carlos said, as it brought a smile to Haley's face brighten up her world.....

Haley wasn't interested in talking she walked over to Carlos trying to suck his dick. Carlos told her no he wanted pussy. Carlos didn't want her to taste Katie's pussy on his dick then she would've known he was cheating. She stood up took her clothes off as Carlos remained on the bed slipping his boxers and t-shirt off. She got on top of him, she placed his dick in her pussy and took him to the Rodeo show.....

Days and nights with no end he tried to figure out how, and when he would be able to end his secret love affair with Katie.....

He sat down and wrote Bo-Diggla explaining to him the situation between him, Katie, and Haley. Bo-Diggla wrote him right back telling him that he got himself in a jam and that he couldn't give him any advice on how he should handle that situation, and that he should've never fucked Katie in the first beginning. Bo-Diggla told him in a joking manner that he should try to do a threesome with Haley, and Katie.....

Carlos began asking Haley for a threesome, but not with Katie of course just in general. Carlos just knew

Haley would say hell no; contrary to his belief Haley said she was interested, the few times she watched porn she liked seeing a big dick going in and out of another woman's pussy. She loved seeing other women getting fucked; and that she'd love to see Carlos fucking another woman that would turn her own. Only problem was that she would be jealous, and she worried about if Carlos would tell someone later on in life. Carlos told her he'd never tell anybody because she was and always will be a reflection of him, and didn't want to say or do anything to make her look bad.

She sat and thought about all the times she'd seen on talk shows how a woman would have a threesome and the man involved with end up leaving his regular lover for the other woman in the threesome or would end up cheating sneaking around with the other woman in the future.....

Haley was interested but didn't give him a definite yes or no.

Carlos began to talk to Katie about a threesome, he just knew she'd say hell no, oh how he was wrong. Katie immediately told Carlos she'd do a threesome but she wouldn't be interested in having sex with her own sister. Carlos told Haley that she wouldn't actually be getting physical with her own sister, that both of them would be having sex with him. Katie said she'd love that, that's the way she wanted it to be since day one her and her sister sharing him with no secret.....

Carlos told Katie she'd have to work on Haley. "First thing to do is when you, and her are alone tell her of fantasies of a threesome," Carlos told Katie.

The next night Katie began to tell Haley of her interest in a threesome. Haley told Katie that she was interested in a threesome, but Haley never told Katie of Carlos interest in a threesome or what was discuss with Carlos in privacy.

As time overlap Katie begin to tell Haley more and more that she wanted a threesome.....

One late night while Carlos was out, and about, Haley and Katie sat at the dinner table as Katie made up a lie saying she she'd accidently bust in on Carlos in the shower and seen his big dick and went to her room for masturbation. "Ever since that night I'd fantasize of Carlos cock in my mouth and pussy. One night I peeped in your room as you and Carlos was having sex and fingered myself as Carlos cock went in and out your Vagina I couldn't believe you could handle it, it's so big," Katie said. Haley didn't reply but instead smirked giggled and got on another subject.....

As they finished eating they loaded the dishes into the dishwasher as Katie got back on the subject. "You, me, and Carlos should have a threesome," Katie said as Haley accidently dropped a plate to the floor as it shattered to pieces. "No Katie I will not have a threesome with my sister, that's disgusting," Haley said. "We're not going to have a sex with one another we will both have sex with Carlos," Katie said. "No Katie not with my sister," Haley said as she got on another subject.....

For weeks with no end Carlos would talk to Haley each night as they laid in the bedroom about a threesome.

One late night unexpectedly as Carlos and Haley laid in the bed, as Haley had just finished sucking his dick she told Carlos that she would do the threesome and that it would have to be with Katie. Carlos mouth and eyes opened up wide in amazement.....

Carlos and Haley walked to Katie's room naked as the day they was born. As they entered Katie's room asshole naked Katie smiled because she knew what time it was.

Haley and Carlos stepped to Katie as she laid in her bed in her panties and bra she immediately took off her panties and bra and laid back in the bed.

As Haley held Carlos dick in her hand she told Katie this is what you wanted so open wide. As Katie continued to lay on the bed Carlos and Haley remained standing as Katie begin eating Carlos dick Haley begin tongue kissing his mouth like never before.

Prior to the whole ordeal Carlos had been smoking weed and popping pills so therefore he was in a total pleasure zone.

In no time Carlos was nutting in Katie's mouth as she swallowed all his nut he took his lips apart from Haley. As Haley and Katie fell to their knees. Haley began sucking his dick as Katie ate his balls all at the same time. The second nut took a little longer but once it came he unleashed it in both of their faces.....

Carlos laid Katie on the bed to fuck right before he put the dick in Haley sucked it briefly, and jagged it off to get hard. Once it was hard Haley placed his dick into Katie's pussy and started fucking the shit out of her, as she moaned in pleasure and in pain Haley stood up fingering herself and playing with her own titties sucking each nipple one by one. Outta nowhere as Carlos continued to fuck Katie, Haley started sucking Katie's titties.....

Afterwards Katie and Haley stood on their feet and begin kissing one another. At first Haley, and Katie wasn't going to have sex with one another but once everything took place they were really feeling themselves.

As Haley and Katie stop kissing Haley got on her knees to starting eating Katie's pussy as Carlos tongue kissed Katie all at the same time. Haley and Katie switched up. Katie got on her knees to eat Haley's pussy as Carlos tongue kissed Haley.....

As time progressed along the initial threesome made all three of their lives great. They'd walk around the house naked having all type of sex with one another.....

In the future that was to come Carlos would marry Haley but promised that he'd still treat Katie as his wife as well he'd treat them both as equals, loving as a sequel.....

Chapter 26

As a couple of years went past. Haley, Katie, and
Carlos remained together. It seemed as it was nothing
or no one that could or would come between them or
tear them apart.....It's as if they lived a periodic time
frame of paradise foot on solid ground but felt as they
were skiing on ice loved each other loved life, the apple,
ripe fruit upright from the tree of life.

One summer's day Carlos was at home alone had been smoking and popping felt high, high as the birds above the clouds, high as airplanes that fly for miles and miles, high as mountain tops and as the Earth goes round, and round and unexpectedly the doorbell rings. He opened the door and this young white lady barged in the house with a suitcase in hand and demanded Carlos to pick up the rest of her luggage.

"Who are you, you sure you got the right house," Carlos asked her? "Yes this is my mother's house didn't she tell you I was coming," she said.....Awwww this is Haley's daughter Rebecca Carlos thought to himself.....

"No she didn't," Carlos said. "Why are you standing there grab my luggage," she said.

Carlos grabbed her luggage and brought it in the house.

He'd sit down and talk to Rebecca her words wasn't very nice she seemed as if she didn't like him.....

Rebecca she was the true essence of a spoiled brat.

"My mom is always speaking highly of you, I can't see what she see in you," Rebecca said. Right then and there Carlos knew him, and Rebecca wouldn't be getting along.....

Shortly Haley came home, and Haley and Rebecca went out to enjoy themselves. Haley offered Carlos to go with them Carlos declined the offer.

For the next several days Carlos was going crazy dealing with Rebecca. He couldn't really have sex with Katie, he couldn't walk around naked and Rebecca was a straight asshole.

Rebecca was on her summer break, Carlos couldn't wait until summer break was over so she could go back to college.

As weeks progressed along Haley, and Katie would go places that didn't include Rebecca therefore Carlos was left to be Rebecca's host, this was a nightmare come true for Carlos.....

One day Rebecca needed Carlos to take her down town shopping. For some reason Rebecca like wearing the clothes that people in the hood wore. Once they made it downtown they went into the store to buy Pelle Pelle leathers. Carlos brought himself a Pelle, a few shirts, and few pair of pants; Rebecca only brought herself a Pelle.

As they paid for their Pelle's and exited the store security started harassing Carlos, looking through his bag to see if he had been shoplifting. Rebecca had been paying attention all along when Carlos wasn't security

had been following Carlos around on the low.

"I understand that you guys must do your job, but

proper procedures is for you to check the receipts then

check the items to match, common law records says

that no one should be discriminated, because of their

sexual preference or of their race, per se," Rebecca said.

Security ignored her and kept harassing, and being

rude to Carlos.....

Rebecca upped her school I.D. that showed she was a

law student.....

"Leave him alone right know before I have my entire

law school down here filing a law suit," Rebecca said.

Through all the commotion the store manager came

out Rebecca showed her, her I.D., and told her about

the problem. The female store manager apologized to

Rebecca and gave Rebecca, and Carlos she free clothes. That's the last thing the store manager wanted was for a bunch of law students that was thirsty for a reputation to come into the store trying to file a law suit.....

After that day Carlos, and Rebecca started to like one another just a little bit.

In time Rebecca would see Carlos high, although he never smoked any weed or popped any pills in front of her she still could tell he was high from the redness, and the tightness of his eyes.

A few times Rebecca would question Carlos on how does it feel to be high, each time Carlos would convert to another subject, he didn't want to turn Rebecca out to getting high.

Rebecca had never got high off anything, never once even sipped any liquor; but she'd see some of her classmates high at parties and they seemed to be really enjoying, feeling themselves as she always wondered how would it feel to be high, but she never tried it.....

Rebecca wanted to feel the stimulation, the art of inhaling, exhaling clouds of smoke to reach a great level of joy, excitement as if she would be walking on clouds....

Rebecca told Carlos time after time she wanted to try smoking weed at least once in life. Time after time Carlos would flip to another subject.....

One day Carlos decided to get her high because he knew if he didn't get her high others would and they'd probably slip something in her drink, or lace her weed.

She told Carlos she wanted to get high but didn't want any addiction. Carlos told her weed isn't like coke or heroin she wouldn't turn into an addict.

Carlos set a blazing fire to the blunt as it sizzled he took two hits, and passed it to Rebecca.

Rebecca hit it once and started choking, and coughing up Saliva. Carlos assumed that would discourage her from wanting to continue to smoke. Oh how he was wrong, she still wanted to smoke. He gave her, a small cup of Champagne. After she took a sip of the Champagne he gave her instruction on her to hit the blunt easy and how to inhale and exhale. It took her a few times to get it right, but once she got it right she felt dizzy at first but afterwards she could feel the pleasure the delight, visions the stars and the Moon that lite up the sky at night; she felt the greatest stimulation, the greatest peace that shall ever be.

After smoking Carlos gave Rebecca a small piece of X-pill she really was feeling herself.....

As days to follow Rebecca turned into a straight sweetheart the weed brought out the best in her.....

Rebecca and Carlos begin to spend more and more time together. Eventually Rebecca began to talk to Carlos more and more about sex, not having sex with her but just in general. She told Carlos she only had sex with two guys in her entire life, one had a little dick, the other had an average size dick. Neither one of them would eat her pussy, but she did suck the guy with the average size dick from time to time although he would never eat her pussy. She'd go on to tell Carlos she couldn't wait to get her pussy ate for the first time. Right then and there Carlos knew she wanted some action in the bedroom.....

Rebecca was attractive but Carlos didn't want to get in a jam by having sex with Rebecca.....

One late night as Rebecca, and Carlos was high as a kite they went to a diner. As they ate and sipped wine Rebecca took off her shoes off and started rubbing it against Carlos leg, he didn't reject it felt good. As they ate and left the diner speechless they held hands as if they'd been lovers forever.....

As they rode in the car peaceful high and quiet listening to a soft rock station they made their way to Motel room. Once in the room there was nothing to talk about they both undressed as Carlos begin tongue kissing her pussy, her love for sex was taking to an all time high. She was high off weed, pills, and had been sipping a little wine and was getting her pussy at be an expert.....

As he continued to eat her pussy at a low tone she'd continue to say Carlos I love you, Carlos I love you, Carlos I love you, non stop at slow, and low tone.....

As he stopped eating her pussy and instructed her to get up he turned her around and bent her over as with her head she slung her long beautiful hair to the side.

As he bent he over a little more he told her to spread her own ass cheeks with her hands, and she did he entered, forced his way in the tight pussy grabbed her shoulders and fucked her hard fast giving her all the dick in it's roughest form.....

When it was almost time to nut he turned her around instructed her to bend down as he gently placed his dick in her mouth she begin sucking on the dick as Saliva ran out her mouth on it as her mouth was fantastic. In no time he was nutting in her mouth as she swallowed every bit of the nut.....

Afterwards he tried to fuck her in the ass but it didn't

work out it would take some time and some fingering.

His dick was to big for a virgin booty.....

Chapter 27

As time overlaps Rebecca and Carlos would spend time together almost everyday. It never once crossed Haley's mind that Carlos and Rebecca was fucking; actually Haley thought that it was a great idea for them to be together because Carlos was her future husband.....

The summer had came to an end it was time for Rebecca to go back to college. Carlos would definitely miss the pussy, but still had Haley, and Katie so everything was all good.....

Once Haley went back to college she'd call Carlos from time to time, not a lot, but at least once a week.....

One day Carlos had been coming home from a hard days work, he stepped in the house and there Rebecca sat with the cutest red lip stick on. Haley and Katie was gone. Rebecca jumped up and kissed Carlos on the lips Carlos panicked because she had on lip stick and he didn't know when Haley or Katie would be making it home. Carlos ran to the bathroom to wash the lip stick off his lips. He ran back downstairs.....

"Where is your mom, and Katie," Carlos asked Rebecca? "They went shopping, they'll be gone for a while," Rebecca said. Carlos knew that was true Haley, and Katie would take forever going shopping.

He took her the bedroom strip her naked and beat the pussy up.....

After fucking they laid in the bed as Rebecca told him she took a flight only for the weekend, and she'd faithfully come to see him every weekend. She had no weekend classes so that wouldn't interfere with her college life.....

For many months Rebecca would come to see Carlos each weekend faithfully. Once again Haley nor Katie suspected a thing.

Carlos felt like a true player, fucking the twin sisters, and the daughter.....

Chapter 28

One night when Carlos, Haley, and Katie had finished

having a threesome Haley begin to discuss with Katie,

and Carlos about Rebecca. Rebecca was two months

pregnant by some Latino guy named Lopez. Lopez was a

dope dealer whom was part of the Mexican Mafia.

Rebecca met Lopez in school. She didn't realize that

Lopez was a dope dealer until they became lovers.
Lopez was only taking college classes to attempt to
confuse the police, and the Feds. Sadly Lopez was killed.
Haley tried to get Rebecca to get an abortion, but
Rebecca said she was keeping her baby.

Carlos knew in the back of his mind that this individual
named Lopez didn't exist, Carlos knew that, that was his
baby.

Then Haley mentioned that Rebecca would be moving
back with them, because Rebecca needed help through
her pregnancy, and that Carlos would make a wonderful
Godfather.

I'm not the Godfather, I'm the real father Carlos
thought to himself.....

Within a couple weeks Rebecca was back at Haley
home to live. Once Carlos got Rebecca alone he told her

congratulations on her pregnancy, "so who's the lucky man." "You know I'd never have sex while you and I was together, I'd never cheat on you, I love you, I can't wait until our baby is born," Rebecca said.

Days to follow Carlos tried his best to convince Rebecca to get an abortion, but she wouldn't do it.

Rebecca told Carlos he could still marry her mom, and that he could be in the child's life as a Godfather.

Carlos told her that that wouldn't work out.

She told Carlos it's only one way to find out.....

After a couple months Rebecca moved in her own apartment approximately 30 minutes away from Haley's home, and ten minutes away from the university. She still would attend college until she was eight months pregnant. Once she was nine months pregnant she would take on-line classes until the baby was born.....

Throughout Rebecca's pregnancy Carlos was supportive of her which made him seem like a great guy in Haley's and Katie's eyes.....

Almost everyday Carlos would enjoy the pregnant pussy.....

Nine months and 21 days the baby was born it was a boy. Rebecca named him Joseph after Mary's husband from the bible.

The new born brought so much joy, to Carlos, Rebecca, Haley, and Katie's life.

Carlos would spend time with his son everyday. The only problem was that he couldn't raise the son like it was his very own. Carlos eventually told his mom, she was happy to have a grandson, Joanne would spend lots of time with Joseph, but Joseph could never know she was his actual grandmother which was sad to Joanne.....

In the beginning the early stages of Joseph's life Haley never suspected Carlos to be Joseph's father, until later on life she started notice that Joseph looked just like Carlos, and Joseph looked as if he was mixed with white and black, not white and Hispanic. Haley just figured that it was a coincidence that Carlos, and Joseph looked alike.

The next day Haley, and Rebecca was by themselves driving to the grocery store. Haley began to ask Rebecca why she'd never introduced Joseph to Lopez family. Rebecca instantly thought of a lie. "I'd never met Lopez family, and I don't even know his real name to contact his family," Rebecca said.

You've been in a relationship, and going to college, and pregnant by a guy and you don't even know his real name or never met his family, that don't sound right Haley thought to herself within her own silent mind.....

Chapter 29

Eleven years past, and Haley, and Carlos was still happily married, Katie still lived with him as she was like Carlos second wife. Rebecca had a prestigious law firm that had a reputation for beating cases. Rebecca had been in two relationships over the course of the eleven years she'd never cheat on the ones she was in the relationship with not even with Carlos. But Carlos could still fuck her if she was single. She was currently single her two exes was black guys; Carlos turned her out to liking black guys.....

As Carlos and Joseph was home alone Carlos thought
that Joseph was asleep. Carlos was sitting back
watching a xxx-rated flick.....

Without Carlos knowing Joseph stood behind him for
ten minutes watching the xxx-rated flick. Carlos begin to
sense someone standing behind him he looked back
and noticed that Joseph was standing behind him
watching the movie.....

Carlos immediately cut the movie off and was going
to discipline Joseph, but decided that this was the best
time to start giving Joseph the player game just as his
dad did him.

"Rule number 1 Joseph never trust a woman under no
circumstances," Carlos said.....

Made in the USA
Las Vegas, NV
07 July 2021